Go And Catch
A Flying Fish

MARY STOLZ

Harper & Row, Publishers

New York   Hagerstown   San Francisco   London

FIRST EDITION

Library of Congress Cataloging in Publication Data
Stolz, Mary Slattery, date
   Go and catch a flying fish.

  "An Ursula Nordstrom book."
  SUMMARY: Taylor, Jem, and B.J. each react
differently to the breakup of their parents'
marriage.
   [1. Family problems—Fiction] I. Title
PZ7.S875854Gn   [Fic]   78-21785
ISBN 0-06-025867-5
ISBN 0-06-025868-3 lib. bdg.

Go And Catch
A Flying Fish

AN URSULA NORDSTROM BOOK

For Jill Harker,
to begin with
and Margie and Bob Sokol,
to go on with

Go And Catch
A Flying Fish

~one

At being what they are without pretension, fish are flawless, but they are not nature's brainiest effort. Nonetheless, those fish that Jem Reddick and his friend Dan Howard went after one summer morning seemed to know precisely the intentions of the two boys. In water up to their waists, Jem and Dan walked slowly and cautiously, each holding a pole at either end of a sixteen-foot seining net equipped with leads at the bottom and floats on the top. They had been here over an hour, dragging near the dock that extended out on the bay from Jem's house, and had only a few pinfish and shiners to show for it.

"Maybe," said Dan, "you shouldn't have let the others go before we got some more, huh? I mean, I was kind of hoping you'd keep the sea horse anyhow. We could've watched him grow up, and maybe seen him get some babies and carry them around in his pouch."

"How could he have some babies if there wasn't any female in there to help him?"

Dan shrugged. "How should I know? I'm not sure how it works with sea horses. I'm not even sure how it works with people."

"I've got a book you can read. Tells you everything."

"No hurry," said Dan, who was interested, but not enough to read a book. "I sure liked that sea horse," he said sadly.

Jem had the best, biggest saltwater aquarium anywhere. He also had what, to Dan, was the unreasonable habit of turning everything in it back into the bay every three weeks. Jem's position was that fish, after all, didn't have such a lot to look forward to, so it was wrong to take what they did have—freedom— away from them except for a little while.

Earlier, he'd released the little sea horse, a pipefish, two four-eye butterfly fish (two real eyes in front, two eye spots toward the back, a device for fooling other fish, who wouldn't know if they were coming or going and so wouldn't know where to grab a bite) and a silver-grey black-striped tophat. Now the aquarium was empty except for a sargassum fish, at present trudging across the bottom on its little armlike fins.

Jem had got him in the bait net the day before when he'd been casting for shiners. He had a bucket now where he was putting baitfish they'd caught in the seine. He planned to go out later, on the bay, and try his luck.

Dan wiped his arm across his forehead and said, "Let's quit, Jem. Let's go out some night and get some."

In the dark, with a Coleman lantern, you could daze the fish and practically scoop them up in your hand. It was great, walking at low tide under the dock, near the rocks, in the dark, the lantern turning the water greeny bright, your feet stirring up phosphorescent particles, fish darting into the light and hanging there almost suspended.

"I don't want to quit," Jem said. "Not before we get something."

But Dan's attention had run its span. He wanted to be off doing something else. Riding his bike, eating something, even looking at television in the middle of the morning. Dan's short attention span angered his father, fussed his mother, exasperated his teachers. They had consultations about it. Once a week, Dan went to a psychiatrist.

"I'm supposed to go to him today," he said now.

"To who?"

"Dr. Borden."

"Oh."

Jem washed the seine down with a hose and the two boys spread it on the dock to dry in the sun.

"What do you talk to him about, Dan?"

"Nothing."

"No, really. I'm curious. Unless you don't want to tell me, of course."

"I don't talk to him."

"Not ever?"

"I guess I said hello Dr. Borden the first day, but not since then."

"So what do you do when you're there?"

"Sit."

"What does he do?"

"He says, 'Do you feel like talking today?' and I shake my head and then we both just sit."

"Jeez. That's flakey. Your father pays for that?"

"Well, sure. I'm there an hour. Fifty minutes, really. Then he looks at his clock and says, 'Time.' And I split."

"What does your father say about it? I mean, doesn't it burn him to pay for you to sit and say nothing every week and he gets bills for it?"

"He doesn't know. Only you do. And Sandy."

"You mean Dr. Borden doesn't tell them?"

"He can't. That's against the rules, for a doctor to tell anything about his patient to anybody. I can tell, but he can't. And I don't. Except you and Sandy."

"He can't tell even if the patient's a kid?"

"Nope."

Jem shook his head. "Boy, what a waste of time."

"What's the diff? I got plenty of time."

"Well then, a waste of money." In Jem's house, money loomed. Spending it, not spending it, wasting it, not wasting it, having it or not having it. Money got talked about a lot.

But Dan just shrugged.

"I guess I'll clean the old seawater out," Jem said. "We can put the sargassum fish in the small tank for a while."

The whole transfer, every three weeks, was a lengthy process, and he liked to have Dan's help.

"You want some pie and milk?" he asked as they hosed their hands and feet, the water running down between the boards of the dock.

"Sure. What kind?"

"Pecan."

"You make it, or Tony?"

"I did."

"Boy, you're something," Dan said admiringly.

Jem, at ten, was as good a cook as his sister, Taylor, who was thirteen, the same age as Dan's sister, Sandy. Both Jem and Taylor could cook better than their mother could. They'd been taught by Tony Reddick, their father, who was night chef at a French restaurant in town.

As they started into the house, Jem halted abruptly

on the threshold. Dan, banging into him, started to protest, then backed hurriedly onto the porch and said in a loud careless voice, "Guess I'll catch that pie later, Jem. Tomorrow, or something. See you."

In the living room, Tony Reddick and his wife, Junie, were yelling at each other.

"Are you absolutely crazy?" Tony bellowed. "What is this thing for?"

"It isn't *for* anything." Jem heard the nervous angry quaver in his mother's voice. He wanted to stop listening to them, but stood and listened. It was that screen they were fighting about. The screen with three panels and some Chinese scenes on it that Junie had got yesterday at an estate sale. She'd brought it home with her in the back of the station wagon and set it up in the living room and stood back, smiling at it and her children.

"Beautiful, isn't it?" she'd said.

Jem and Taylor had looked at each other. Their mother was forever buying things that their father said they could not afford. Fights went on about it all the time. Well, a lot of the time. Junie went to tag sales and auctions and estate sales, and she could never go to a sale without buying something. Not always a big or expensive thing. But always, Tony said, something they didn't need and couldn't afford.

Jem thought that what she bought was usually

pretty. Like the set of fruit knives and forks with gold handles she'd got a couple of months ago.

"Who uses those things anymore?" Tony had shouted. "And what do we need with a set of twenty-four if we did use them?"

She bought incomplete sets of beautiful china with lots of chips. And worn-out Oriental rugs. Once a bronze and marble clock that no one could repair. She'd bought a marquetry coffee table, inlaid with mother-of-pearl. That time Tony had thrown a plate across the room and by the time it smashed against the wall he'd had the table in his hands and would have thrown it, too, if Junie hadn't hurled herself at him like a mother protecting her child. It was in the living room now, piled with so much stuff—books, magazines, ashtrays, a bowl of flowers, a backgammon set, a wooden bird—that you couldn't see the mother-of-pearl design. The old table was up in Taylor's room.

Apparently, getting in late and sleeping pretty late as he sometimes did, their father hadn't noticed the screen until just now.

"It is not *for* anything," Junie repeated shakily. "It's just something beautiful. It's a Chinese coromandel screen and valuable. It's worth far more than—" She broke off.

"All right," said Tony. "Tell me. I want to know what the beautiful thing cost, and I want to know now, and I don't want any lies."

"Don't you talk to me that way. I'm not a slavey—yours or anyone else's."

"If there's someone in slavery around here, sister, it isn't you. Who's faced with bills piling up everywhere, dunning letters in every mail, and who has to pony up for all this junk you find at junk sales?"

"I do not buy junk," Junie said icily. "Name one thing I've ever bought that wasn't beautiful. Look at that screen. Put your *eyes* on it and *see* it. It's a fine and handsome piece that you won't find duplicated anywhere."

"Handsome is as handsome does and that thing's done me out of plenty, I'll bet. How much did it cost?" Silence. "Junie, how much did you spend on it?"

"Have I ever spent so much that you couldn't afford it?"

"I haven't had to take out a second mortgage, if that's what you mean. Not yet. Will you tell me what it cost!" Silence again from Junie. "Okay. Okay, I'm going to take it back—where did you say you got it?"

"I didn't say, and I won't. And don't you call me sister, Buster."

"I'll find out, believe me. I'll phone your friend Bette Danziger, who can afford to throw her husband's money away—"

"Her husband's money. You make me sick. *Husband's* money. I thought marriage was a partnership.

Isn't that what you told me when you wanted so badly to have me for a partner? Isn't it? A partnership—I can hear your voice saying it. Share and share alike. Everything. Sex and housework and joy and woe—remember saying words to that effect, Tony?"

"I remember. I guess I didn't realize you'd do your best to run the partnership into bankruptcy—"

"Tony, you can't humiliate me in front of Bette Danziger. You just can't. Anyway, they don't take stuff back at estate sales." She was beginning to sound tearful. "Maybe I can try to sell it myself—"

To Jem, it sounded pretend-pitiful, but Tony always seemed to fall for it. He groaned and said, "Ah, Junie, please . . . try to understand, won't you? I don't want to deprive you of things—"

Jem walked slowly to the end of the dock, biting the edge of his thumbnail. He sat down and watched a darting slivery school of shiners in the water beneath him. He looked at brown pelicans diving out on the bay. They shot with tremendous explosions of water into a wide area churned by schooling pinfish, or maybe grunts. The pelicans were being bullied by sea gulls. Oceangoing pickpockets, the sea gulls. Pickbills? They were capable of taking the fish right out of a pelican's mouth. Jem liked pelicans. They were the only birds he knew of that occasionally took a day off. All other birds left the roost, the perch, the nest, whatever, at dawn and got about the business of finding something to eat. But the pelican would, from time to time, wake up on his perch among the mangroves, look around, shift, say to himself, "Oh, I just can't." Then he'd tuck his head beneath his wing and just go back to sleep. Neat.

That screen was pretty. As the coffee table was. And the clock that wouldn't go. Most of the junk Junie brought home was pretty. And when Junie cried, Tony stopped yelling. They must have stopped because he couldn't hear them anymore. Sometimes he figured you could hear them clear across the bay to Wrasse Island. Now they were making up, he guessed. When Junie cried, the next step was Tony begged her to stop, and then it got around to kissing. Once Jem had wondered if they didn't like fighting, they seemed to have such a smoochy time making up. Make that used to have? Did they make up in the old way so much anymore? How could you really tell with grown-ups? You couldn't be around them all the time. Besides, they had ways of pretending that he, anyway, couldn't keep straight in his head. "Let's pretend" was supposed to be a kid's game. Jem, looking at the adults in his world, wondered if anyone ever outgrew it.

Tony said she'd bankrupt them. Sometimes he'd yell that she'd have them all in the poorhouse. Was there such a place as a poorhouse? Tony had laughed when he asked and said no and don't worry, things would work out. "It'll work out somehow," Tony had assured him.

"Things always do."

Jem wondered if that was so.

Junie was beautiful. She was like a garden. She'd run along the beach with a kite string and get a kite into the air in seconds flat if there was a breeze at all. She looked like a girl, speeding down the sand in her bikini. Jem wished she'd wear a sort of cape or something, unless she was in the water. Guys whistled at her. Not just men. Kids his own age, some of them took a look at Junie and said, "Wow!" It was nice to have a beautiful mother, but sometimes—he hunched a little—sometimes he wondered if it'd be maybe easier to have a mother like Dan's. Mrs. Howard wore stockings even in the summertime. Jem didn't think *his* mother owned a pair of stockings.

A sonic boom shook the air. Jem looked up angrily. Jets from one of the airports over on the west coast. He hated them. They disturbed fish, scared birds, broke windows, troubled the atmosphere. They were not supposed to break the sound barrier, but did it and got away with it. In spite of people writing letters and signing petitions.

People asked kids what they wanted to be when they grew up. Dumb question. Nosy. Still, people asked. Jem didn't know what he wanted to be, but knew plenty of things he was not planning on. He did not want to be some guy in the sky breaking the sound barrier. He didn't want to be a policeman, or in the service. He didn't want to be a lawyer or a doctor or a certified accountant. Or a credit to anybody.

Grandmother Reddick, Tony's mother, who visited two or three times a year from Lexington, Massachusetts, was hot for people being credits to other people. She had rules to make this possible, if you followed them.

Grandmother Reddick: Tony, the children behave more like savages every time I come. Their manners are terrible, they run around practically naked, they eat the eyeballs of fish—

Tony: Oh, come on, Mother. They're great kids.

Grandmother Reddick: I do not deny that. I love them as much as you do and I'm speaking for their good.

Tony: Well, I think their manners are okay. And fish eyes taste fine, once you develop the taste.

Grandmother Reddick: Tony, you are trying to annoy me.

Tony: Oh no. I don't want to annoy anybody. Believe me.

Grandmother Reddick: You *were not brought up to eat fish eyes.*

Tony: Maybe that's why I moved to Florida. I drove and I drove, looking for a little town with small houses and big trees where I could be uncomfortable from the heat most of the year, and I found it and I love it. And the kids love it. It's good for them to run around practically naked. The fish eyes are a bonus.

Grandmother Reddick: All right. You love Florida, and we'll dismiss the topic of fish eyes for good. But these children have no routine, and children need routine. They want it. Yours have none. *Their bedtime hours are a disgrace.*

Tony: They don't have any bedtime hours.

Grandmother Reddick: Don't fence with me, Tony.

Tony: You know something, Mother? I remember lying awake in the dark, trying like hell to go to sleep. I don't want my children doing that.

Jem and Taylor stayed out of their grandmother's way as much as possible during her visits. It wasn't that they didn't like her. They did, in a way. And

Taylor said that she *was* saying those things for their own good. Just the same—they avoided her. B.J., their little brother, was crazy about her. Which was, Junie said, very nice for Grandmother Reddick. She didn't add nice for the rest of them. Ever since B.J. had got old enough to notice Grandmother and fall in love with her, she'd paid most of her attention to him. Her tolerance for boredom where he was concerned was endless. She could read the same book to him six times a day every day for as long as her visit lasted and not lose that enthusiastic reading tone. She played Go Fish by the hour, sat with him while he constructed space cities with his Lego set, and exclaimed happily over his crayonings, although Tony said he'd rarely encountered a child with less talent in the field.

Jem clasped his arms across his chest and stared at the diving birds. Sunlight sparkled on the bay. Penny-water, his father called it.

His parents had fights, his grandmother had standards, and they were all grown-up. When people asked what he wanted to be when he grew up, Jem usually answered, "A tarpon with a human brain." That shut them up. One thing he did not want to be, when the time came, was married. He guessed what he didn't want was to be grown-up at all.

Taylor, in her room at the top of the house, was

working on her life list of birds. So far, it included only species seen in Florida, since the farthest from home she'd ever been was the Everglades. A person could spend all her life in the Everglades and not want for interest, but Taylor's ambitions were worldwide. Every bird in the world was what she asked to see. Even Roger Tory Peterson had only sighted half.

She was trying now to decide if she should strike from her list the black-necked stork she'd seen last winter in Shark Valley. It had certainly been a sighting. It had equally certainly been an escapee from a zoo, and therefore not a legitimate candidate for anyone's life list of wild birds. There were no black-necked storks native to Florida, or even to the Western Hemisphere. A stork, of course, could fly thousands of miles, but none had been known to fly from Africa to Miami. She had put it on her list, last February, because—she now acknowledged—of a wish to pad it. Now she frowned, drew a line across it and wondered if she shouldn't start a notebook of accidentals and casuals. Birds spotted in Florida that did not belong in Florida.

She poked around her bookshelves but could not come up with a fresh notebook, so she'd have to get one sometime soon. Or find one somewhere in the house. If you could pick your way through the clutter, you could turn up practically anything in their house.

Her room was an octagon on the roof, with windows on four of the sides. On the four wall sides were posters of birds. A great horned owl and her chicks. A bald eagle baby perched on the side of his great nest, the down still showing under his wings and his bloomers blowing in the breeze. A beautiful flock of avocets. A Mexican azure-browed mot-mot. She had never seen an azure-browed mot-mot in the wild but to know one existed made her feel good. She supposed that with the hideous trade in wild birds that went on all over the world, they might be extinct by the time she got old enough to go to Yucatan and look for one. Thirteen now. She could probably take off on her own by the time she was eighteen. Five years. A long time. In five years a lot of extinction could go on, and the azure-browed mot-mot might be among the victims. People were crazy, people were cruel—wanting to put wild birds in cages. To show off. Prove, probably, that they had enough money to get a wild bird. Like a hyacinth macaw, from South America. Some man she'd read about had paid $9,000 for a hyacinth macaw to put in his huge atrium in his huge house. The bird had died. What else could it do but die, taken from the Amazon jungle, flown in an airplane to a place called Harrison, New York, put in an atrium for people to look at while they drank *piña coladas*, probably, to put them in a jungly mood? Under the circumstances what could a hyacinth macaw do except die?

Junie and Tony were yelling at each other down in the living room. "Screen scene," Taylor said to herself. She must remember to say it to Jem. She'd wait, though, to go down and search for a notebook.

She sat on the window seat of her tower room and looked across the water that today was prickly bright. Out there, far away but easily brought close by her telescope (Christmas and birthday present combined, secondhand, very good), was a mangrove island weighty with nesting pelicans, cormorants, egrets, herons. Crowded at one end, ostracized for their wicked ways, was a colony of the darkly handsome frigate birds. At mating time, in a summoning mood, the gular pouches of the males would swell into huge scarlet beacons, and seen at dusk, if you didn't know what you were looking at, it seemed a celebration of red balloons. Which, as a matter of fact, it was. The brilliant displays that male birds put on to attract mates were over. Now there were eggs, nestlings, fledglings. The mangrove island was in constant winged movement as parents arrived with food, changed places, departed to fish again. Only at night would the island be almost still. Even then, not quite. Sometimes she and Jem took the skiff out and when they neared the island would cut the motor and drift in the dark, and in there among the thick-limbed, heavily crowned mangroves there would be soft sounds, rustlings, shrill baby peeps.

Junie was crying now. Last time they'd had a battle this prolonged it had ended with Tony tearing out of the house, pulling their Sunfish, *Merrywing,* into the water and heading out for the Gulf of Mexico. He'd been gone a couple of hours and had just beat a storm home. By the time he'd hauled *Merrywing* back on the beach, with Jem's help, the sky was roiling black, bursting at the seams with thunder, torn to bits with pale slashes of lightning. And until he made it back, Junie had stood at the end of the dock, her skirt and long hair whipped by the wind, searching the water with Taylor's binoculars and saying, over and over, "Oh please, oh please . . ."

Crazy people, both of them.

Her brother was at the end of the dock, kicking his legs, biting his thumb. He and Dan Howard had been dragging for fish earlier, for Jem's aquarium, but apparently hadn't caught anything but baitfish. Dan was gone. Scared off, Taylor supposed, by the shouting. His parents did not shout. Mr. Howard looked (!) like a right jolly old elf, didn't raise his voice and wouldn't permit his wife to. But then, Mrs. Howard never seemed to want anything that her husband would not permit. They had three children. Dan, plump and hyper. Sandy, plump and mellow. Amanda, slender and spaced out on rage. Tony called the Howards "the autocrat and the acolyte of the cocktail table." They drank a bit, but not so as to interfere with the enormous and unrelenting attention they paid to their children.

A little blue heron came around the seawall, taking measured slow strides in the shallow water. Slender and dainty, slatey-blue plumage shining in the sun, he stood and eyed the prospect before him. Then, head thrust forward, he recommenced his walk. On pilings in the water cormorants rested, their wings outspread to dry. They were dark and still as cutout silhouettes. A royal tern shot into the water, emerged with a tiny silvery fish in his bill and flew into an Australian pine with his catch.

Birds seemed so right with themselves. Quarrelsome, some of them. Some with bad habits, like those laughing gulls out there, making life hard for pelicans. Frigate birds and owls were robbers of nests. Frigates sometimes even robbed their own, something no owl would do. Starlings, unlike wood storks and Everglades kites, had never heard of planned parenthood. But no matter how they fussed or misbehaved, it seemed to Taylor that there was no mix-up within themselves about what they were and why they did what they had to do.

Most of the people she knew, grown-ups and kids alike, seemed to be in a condition of tumult all the time. Not Sandy Howard. So what was wrong with Sandy, that she wasn't mixed up?

A plane broke the sound barrier with a tremendous

boom. On the dock, Jem looked angrily at the sky, trying to see where the plane was, so he could take its number and report it. He never managed to do this, since they were always long gone by the time the explosions they caused took place. Probably the thing was from the Naval Air Station at Pensacola, but of course they'd never admit it.

Downstairs, B.J., who'd been napping, screamed into the living room trailed by his yelping Labrador, Drum. The fighting stopped while Junie and Tony comforted B.J. Drum, safe with people all around him, grew quiet. B.J. was brave as a lion about things that lots of kids of four found frightening. Water, strangers, the dark. But loud noises scared him and his dog into hysterics. Thunderstorms, sirens, sonic booms. Domestic uproars didn't bother him. Probably he'd got used to them.

Sonic booms and domestic explosions. Could be the title of a rock song, thought Taylor.

~~two

Their house was cypress-sided, sleek and pewter-colored, like driftwood. "It could be a dwelling washed up by the sea," Junie said. The living room and kitchen and big screened porch took up the front of the first floor, with the bedroom and bath shared by Jem and B.J. at the back. A cluttered house, the Reddicks'. Walls storied with books, hung with pictures, picked out here and there with plaques and masks, a candelabrum, some shadow boxes. Tables almost unusable for the bowls of flowers, shells, for books and magazines and games, scrimshaw and whittled figures, ashtrays for Junie's countless cigarettes. On wide-board floors were worn rag rugs and a couple of Junie's faded Oriental finds. A fieldstone fireplace at one end. In winter it could hold a log big enough to burn all day. There were niches in the mantel above for ginger jars, a Buddha, a carved stone cat. The chairs and sofas were aged leather or velvet, weathered to indistinct hues and clawed by the cat to fringiness. At the other end from the hearth was a round dining table with a center pedestal, its clawed feet clutching brass balls. A large wooden fan hung above the table, and in summer it revolved slowly all day.

A dock extended from the kitchen, its boards washed grey by rain, baked by sun, streaked with salt. Some of the pilings were eroded to stalactites. Jem kept a stone crab farm in the waters underneath. Cinder blocks in which the beautiful ivory-and-rose-colored crabs hovered, their black-tipped claws on the ready for passing pinfish, for scraps that Jem provided. At the end of the dock were some old chairs and a table. They ate there unless the weather, or the mosquitoes, were too bad.

They had a little sailboat they called *Merrywing* that could be pulled up on the sand beside the canoe. Jem's skiff, nameless, rode in the water, the anchor holding it on the dock, fastened at the other end to a piling a few feet off in the bay. Their catboat, *Loon*, was moored at the dock's end.

Behind the house was a shell drive and beyond that about ten untended acres. Great live oaks grew there, air plants and tampanzi orchids and resurrection ferns clustered in their branches, grey Spanish moss dangling down in beards. There were citrus trees and avocados and mangoes, and lots of the beautiful sea grape with leaves like great dinner plates, green in summer, brown in winter. There were fig trees, and banyans, pine trees and palms—reclinata and coconut and date and royal. There were flame trees and jacarandas, and banana trees with huge oar-shaped leaves and clusters of sweet fingerling fruits. And there were flowers— frangipani, hibiscus, oleanders and allamandas, azaleas and gardenias. Birds nested on the ground, in the bushes, in the treetops. Racoons and rattlesnakes and lizards produced their young and tended or forgot them as instinct ordained.

Instinct, too, led real estate agents and land developers to covet this house and its ten acres. They sent letters explaining that price was no object, why not let them come and talk it over, toss the notion around, see what surfaced. "The cement hand of progress, trying to crush our world," Tony would say. Constantly faced with money problems, Tony and Junie nevertheless threw these letters in the wastebasket, unopened. If someone telephoned for the purpose of making an appointment Junie, or Tony, would say, "Sorry, I'm going to hang up on you," and did.

Taylor, still in her room, was listening to the bamboos that grew up past her window. A breeze or a wind caused the high frondy heads to sigh, the hollow stems to creak and click against one another. She was wondering if bamboos grew in rain forests when her father called up the stairs, "Lunch, Taylor!"

They ate at the end of the dock. Spinach salad with bean sprouts, avocado slices, tomato slices, walnuts. Everything except the walnuts homegrown. Two kinds of dressing, homemade bread, pears and iced tea. Gingersnaps, made by Jem.

Taylor forked up a small piece of spinach and looked at it before putting it in her mouth. She chewed slowly.

"Taylor, you aren't eating," Tony said. "You aren't eating well lately at all. Do you feel all right?"

"Sure. I'm just not awfully hungry. Too hot, I guess."

"Heat never stopped you from eating before."

Taylor took another mouthful, swallowed some tea. It was true, and she didn't know why, but even the delicious food that was normal fare at their table didn't tempt her. She wondered if a person could get tired of eating.

"Where's Dan?" Junie asked. "I thought he was going to have lunch with us, Jem."

"He had something he had to do. See his shrink, I guess."

"Psychiatrist," said Tony. "Not shrink."

"Whatever. He had to go."

Taylor guessed why. It was peculiar about Junie and Tony, how they never seemed to think anyone heard them carving up each other. When it was over, and all around them people were feeling like chewed strings, they were calm as could be. Like now, smiling at each other, at their children. Tony ruffled Drum's head, asked Jem what he got new for the aquarium, asked what his family was going to do this afternoon and listened to the answers. Was it all a put-on, designed to disguise their real feelings? How could anyone tell?

"I'm going fishing," Jem said.

"I'm going to bike over to the beach and swim."

"Me too?" B.J. shouted at Taylor. "Me too, Taylor? Can I and Drum go with you?"

"You can. You know Drum isn't allowed on the beach."

"But I want him!"

"You can't have him. You want him to be taken to the pound and then we have to pay a fifty-dollar fine to get him back?"

"Why *can't* he go to the beach?" B.J. demanded.

"Oh, B.J. You know why. Dogs aren't allowed on the beach because they might bite people. And they make poops and people step on it. It's against the law, that's all, to take dogs to the beach."

"But he *wants* to come."

"He can't, so pipe down. We'll build a sand castle."

She turned to her mother. "Could you come with us and fly a kite?"

"Oh darling, I'm sorry. Bette Danziger is coming by. There's an auction over on the mainland she wants to go to. She's still looking for a corner hutch." Tony's mouth tightened, and Junie's long dark eyes narrowed. "I am only going to keep her company, Tony. That's all. I have no intention of buying a thing."

Were they getting worse? Taylor wondered. If it wasn't money, it was why the house was such a mess. If it wasn't the mess or the money, it was why Tony worked such horrible hours that he never had time for his family, never had time for *fun*. If it wasn't money or mess or time or fun it was something else.

If it took two to tangle, you could count on Junie and Tony to make a pair. Jem was nibbling at his nails. He only bit his thumbs. They were gross, chewed way below the quick. Taylor clasped her own thumbs with her fingers. Not that she bit her nails. Not that that was a guarantee against starting. The only guarantee was no guarantee.

She and B.J. rode over to the Gulf side of the island on her bike, taking a shovel, some plastic pails and a kite.

"Kite first or castle first?" she asked.

"Get the kite up, Taylor, and let it fly around and watch us while we do the castle, okay?"

"Okay."

Taylor took off down the beach, arms high, wrists turning as deftly as her mother's. The long narrow strip of crimson and yellow fabric sprang skyward without preliminary flops and flounderings. Even with such a breeze as she had today, some people couldn't get a kite in the air, but Taylor had been taught by an expert. In moments she had it undulating above them, in the domain of the osprey and the frigate bird.

She walked back to B.J., who was cheering and shouting, leaned over and wound the string around a rock and left the kite on its fluttering own. It dove and shimmered and skimmed in great arcs, showing no sign of plunging earthward.

The Reddicks, besides being adroit kite flyers, were skilled sand castle builders, but with only two of them, Taylor didn't plan on anything elaborate.

"How about," she asked, sitting back on her heels, "a moat, an entrance gate, a tower at each corner of the wall, and then a single keep inside? That should keep us busy for a while."

They worked together peacefully. And the ocean, too, was peaceful. It lipped the shore with small foam-crocheted waves. A snowy egret walked at the water's edge, black-stockinged, yellow-booted, plumes ruffling in the onshore breeze. A ghost crab, pale as sand, almost translucent, fixed them with his stalked black eyes, then dashed for a nearby hole and was gone. The ghost crab was capable of courage. In time of peril, if

27

he'd wandered too far from his hole—from any hole, for that matter—he would turn, lift his right claw, pop his black eyes and attempt to terrorize a predator of any size. Taylor had seen a ghost crab face up to Drum and drive him off, probably through the sheer sassiness of the action. Fiddler crabs, too. Taylor had seen the flats at low tide carpeted with thousands of fiddler crabs . . . tiny, tiny, with only one claw each and all those thousands of claws clicking as the little crabs scrambled, making a sound like rain on a tin roof. These, too, would wheel with their pigmy claws held high and defy a seeming enemy a thousand times larger than themselves.

Marvelous, marvelous, the creatures of the earth and sea.

The sand where they were was damp and wonderfully packable. Using the largest pail for the keep, they worked steadily. Once in a while, not often anymore, the entire family came over here to the beach and built castles so elaborate that a picture of one had appeared in the local newspaper. That memorable structure had covered an area Tony said had to be twenty feet square. Four towers in the keep, connected by bridges, encircled by a fosse, a double wall surrounding the whole, with a series of defense towers in the outer one, then a moat and a drawbridge. They'd added all sorts of outbuildings within the walls—guardrooms, storehouses, assembly halls.

There'd been a secret passage leading from the keep to a point outside the fortification. It had taken hours and had been infinitely crenellated, palisaded, decorated. B.J. had brought little flags to surmount the towers of the keep, and his collection of tiny animals with which to people the castle.

As it grew, more and more people had come to watch, to exclaim, to take pictures and, of course, to make the acme dumb remark, "But what a pity the tide will take it away." Taylor, talkative with her family or friends, was taciturn with strangers. She never looked up while her parents answered the comments and posed for the newspaper photographer. She leaned over her part of the structure, lank tan hair falling so it hid her eyes, and wished the people away.

This was what she liked. Summer, with a kite flying overhead and no one nearer than half a mile down the beach where some condominiums were.

A pair of skimmers went by, low over the water, fishing. From a distance they looked black and moved their wings in an odd mechanical way, making them appear unreal, like bats on wires in Halloween plays. Then, as they approached and sped past, just on the waves' surface, white undersides flashing, black and red bills excellently arranged for scooping, they seemed to Taylor to have great elegance. With the possible exception of starlings and doves, there was no bird Taylor did not admire. Some she loved. The sight of an owl, flying softly as a great brown moth through the woods at dusk, made her dizzy with joy. Or a kingfisher perched on a wire above a lake, on a branch over the bay, flashing into the water and out like a tiny arrow.

Only a few yards away from the slowly emerging sand castle, peeps on their pinwheel legs trooped down the beach and trooped right back again. Over and over. Tall among them, willets went their demure and adorable way. For half an hour now an osprey had been hunting back and forth in her view. She heard, every now and then, its flutelike whistle. Twice it had closed its wings and plunged, twice come out of the water, a fish in its talons, and had headed for some feeding perch out of sight. If she had had her binoculars with her, she could have fixed her gaze on his face, his white, black-patched, keen, piratical face. But she hadn't brought her glasses. Time at the beach with B.J. did not allow for bird-watching.

They worked, crenellating the wall, then digging a moat around it. The kite flew above them in the breeze, plunging now and then but just for fun and always rising again. Taylor and B.J., too, went plunging now and then into the lazily lifting clear waters of the Gulf of Mexico.

Now and then the shadows of fleets of pelicans crossed the sand, like shadows of little airplanes.

"What're you smiling for?" B.J. demanded.

"I feel good. I love the summer and the sunshine and the birds and you. I'm happy."

"Oh." B.J. lay on his side to study the castle from a different angle.

"Hey, look," said Taylor. "Here comes Sandy. She has Viva with her."

B.J. scowled horribly. "She is not supposed to take that Viva to the beach." He pointed to a sign. "See that sign? It says NO DOGS ALLOWED ON BEACH."

"It says UNLAWFUL TO PICK SEA OATS."

"Why can Sandy have that Viva here if I can't have Drum?"

"Well, she shouldn't. But just the same, Drum is about forty times bigger. He could swallow Viva like a puppy biscuit."

B.J. smiled. "Could, couldn't he?"

Viva, released from Sandy's arms, came shrilling across the sand toward them.

"Doesn't even sound like a dog," said Taylor. "Sounds more like a sea gull."

To B.J.'s joy, Viva came hurtling right at him. He dropped to his knees and looked adoringly into the tiny face and pop eyes. "Isn't she cute? Isn't she the cutest little *thing*?"

Sandy, at a slower pace, followed her dog. Put one way, she was plump. Put another, she was fat. She had a glorious disposition, a gorgeous complexion, and what Junie called dangerous eyes.

31

Taylor: How do you mean, dangerous?

Junie: Those long dark eyes, the color of es-presso, with long dark lashes like silk fringe. The kind that get their owners and all sorts of other people into deep trouble.

Taylor: How?

Junie: Oh, Taylor. Forget I said anything. Anyway, Sandy's safe. She's too fat to be dangerous.

Taylor: You have to be thin to be danger-ous?

Junie: In the Western world. She'd be the hit of a harem, I daresay.

"Hi," said Sandy, plopping on the sand beside them. "That your kite? I knew it. Hey, this's a neat castle. There's nobody at your house. I phoned and nobody answered."

"Tony's gone to work and Junie's off looking for a corner hutch with Mrs. Danziger."

"You haven't got a corner left to stick a hutch in."

"It's for one of Mrs. Danziger's corners."

"It was Jem I was looking for. I mean, Dan, really. My mother's in a fantod because she can't find him. He go somewhere with Jem?"

"Not now. The two of them dragged for fish for a

while and then Dan left. I thought he was going home."

"Was he on his bike?"

"Yes. What's the matter?"

"Nothing's the *matter*. It's just that Dan's always forgetting what he's supposed to be doing and where he's supposed to be. Drives my mother bananas. She's the one has to face up to *him* when things go wrong. My father," she added unnecessarily. "They have to pay for the hour even if Dan doesn't show and he's missed twice lately. The headshrinker."

"Do you think he's doing Dan any good?" Taylor asked curiously.

"*Quien sabe?* I don't know why they picked Dan, anyway, to get shrunk. I mean, I've obviously got problems, too."

"Maybe yours is just that you eat too much."

"A person eats too much for all kinds of kinky reasons. I just don't understand why they don't want to look around for my loose bolts. Or Amanda's. That girl needs help."

"Maybe they're going to do you one at a time."

"Starting with the youngest? No, it's because Dan's the boy. Amanda and I are prisoners in a pre-feminist household. Oh, and Mother, too, but she digs shackles. Oh well, it'll all be grist for my mill one day."

Sandy was going to be a novelist. In preparation, she did quite a lot of writing, but mostly she read.

33

She read everything, everywhere, under all circumstances. She read in the bathtub, on the beach, beside her swimming pool, on the school bus, in the back seat of her parents' cars. She read while she walked from room to room, or along the sidewalk. At school, during lunch, she sat with a book propped in front of her. Usually something unsuitable disguised by a suitable jacket. She'd read the entire *Valley of the Dolls* with an M.K. Rawlings cover around it. She had a tote bag with her now, and Taylor didn't have to ask to know that some book considered R or even X was safely tucked inside.

"Besides," Sandy went on, "I think it would be interesting, being shrunk. Emmy Lyons is being."

"I know. She tells everybody."

"Did she tell you about talking to herself?"

Taylor shook her head.

"*Well.* This doctor of hers told her to look in a mirror and talk to herself for five minutes every day."

"Weird."

"Isn't it?"

"Does she do it?"

"She told me she tried once. She sat there looking at herself and then *whispered*—she says she couldn't make herself talk out loud—whispered 'Hello?' to this girl in the mirror and then she burst into tears."

"Then what?"

"I don't know. She didn't tell me any more. Do you want to hear something really gross?"

"Sure."

"Amanda says—from reading those magazines about how to make the best of yourself in spite of yourself—that those models, you know, that you see in *Vogue* and on billboards and all, some of them do the *grossest* things to make themselves stay skinny."

"Well, what?"

"Yuck. Well—it seems that Amanda read that some of them can't *keep* from eating, but they aren't supposed to weigh over a hundred pounds even if they're six feet tall. So what these characters do is they eat all they want and then stick their fingers down their throats and *make* themselves barf. Isn't that disgusting?"

"It sure is. I don't see why you have to tell me things like that."

"You asked."

"I should think they'd still be hungry."

"Not according to Amanda. It's the eating that matters, not the digesting."

"Sounds flakey."

"Amanda told me because she thought I should try it. I told her no way. I think I'll go in the water. B.J., watch Viva for me. If you see a cop coming, holler."

She walked off, a bundle of smooth firm fat, honey-colored, and was presently splashing happily in the waves. Taylor peered in the tote bag. *Greenwillow*, by B.J. Chute. She opened the book. *Fear of Flying*. Erica Jong. Taylor read a paragraph, put Ms. Jong back in the tote.

"Come on, B.J. Let's go in the water."

"What about Viva?"

"She can come in if she wants to."

But the ocean was too big for Viva's store of courage. She yapped defiance from the shore.

∾three

When Taylor and B.J. got home, they found Jem on the dock, tying up the skiff, a pail of mullet beside him.

B.J., who could count to ten, counted ten fish and then started over again, counting to three. "That comes to lots, doesn't it?" he said to his brother.

"More than I want to clean. Thirteen, it comes to."

Taylor got a knife from a storage bin on the porch, a thin, sharp fisherman's knife, and settled beside her brother. Together they gutted, scaled and filleted, putting the heads in one bucket, fillets in another. Attracted by the activity, a big blue heron sailed to a landing on the end of the dock, then made a cautious but firm approach. Jem and Taylor and B.J. were sure it was the same heron who arrived and poised within a few feet of them whenever they cleaned fish. A platoon of brown pelicans floated in silent urgency on the waters below. Gulls, laughing and herring, tossed frantically in the air above.

"Throw some to Benjamin," B.J. instructed Jem, pointing at the big blue.

"Since when is he Benjamin?" Taylor asked.

"He's named for Benjamin Bunny. I just did it for him."

"Very suitable," said Taylor. She tossed a length of entrails toward the heron, who tried for it but missed as a laughing gull intercepted and made off across the bay, the intestine trailing like a streamer. Most of the other gulls set off in pursuit, screaming abuse.

B.J. looked sadly at Benjamin. "You didn't try hard enough. Can he have another try?"

"Here, catch!" said Jem, tossing a fish head. This time Benjamin was successful. He caught the head and they watched as it went a visible course down his slender neck. The heron gulped, ruffled his feathers, then drew one leg up and out of sight. Preparing to digest, maybe. The gulls returned, the pelicans paddled about, gazing up mournfully, accepting with dignity what scraps came their way.

As Jem and Taylor worked, blood spread, scales glistened like mounds of sequins on the wooden flooring of the deck. Their cat, Tut, appeared from under the house and crouched, munching on a mullet skin, head tipped to one side, eyes slitted against sunlight flashing on the water. Drum, who did not eat mullet heads or skins, lay on his side under the porch swing, getting as much shade as he could.

When they finished, Jem turned the hose on, washing the fish, their hands, legs, the dock. Blood, scales, fins washed down between the boards.

"Help me feed the crabs, B.J." he said.

"Okay."

They walked halfway down the dock, kneeled and leaned over, looking into the cement block apartment where the stone crabs lived. Jem could never be sure how they knew when he was here above them. Maybe they saw his shadow, or heard his footstep. Whatever, they always came out of hiding when he brought food. He tossed some entrails to the pelicans, to divert them while he dropped a few heads to the crabs, who tiptoed sideways on their delicate legs, snatched at the food with big pincers and backed hurriedly into their cement rooms to chew in privacy.

The telephone rang as Taylor was wrapping the fillets in aluminum foil. "B.J.," she called, "if you get that, don't say just a minute and hang up, hear me?"

"I'll take it," said Jem. In a moment Taylor heard his "Oh, hi, Dan. Yeah, thirteen mullet. . . . Thanks a heap, but Taylor and I have already cleaned them. . . . Wait'll I ask her." He came to the kitchen door. "Dan. He says his father's going to have a cook-out and do we want to come. He says come over now and we can practice diving."

"Fine with me."

"What about Junie? When's she getting back?"

"I don't know. We'll leave her a note."

"I'm going to tell Dan we'll bring the mullet fillets. They're always asking us over there and we never have anyone here."

"We can take some of Tony's rolls, too, tell them."

"Great."

"I have to have a shower first. You two take the stuff and go on over. Tell Sandy I'll be there in a bit."

When Taylor came out of the shower, toweling her hair, the telephone rang again. This time it was her mother, who explained that she and Mrs. Danziger were going to stay in town for a bite and then go to the movies.

"We're going to Sandy's," Taylor said. "Mr. Howard is having another cookout."

"Darling, isn't that nice for you."

"Yes. Except that we go there an awful lot, and we never have them here."

"Honey. Dan and Sandy just about live with us."

"I meant—"

"I know what you meant. But you can't expect me to try to keep up with the Howards. They'd expire on a visit to our house. Only two bathrooms? No swimming pool at *all*? My dear, where's your *help*, surely you didn't prepare this feast all on your little *own*?"

"They aren't that bad."

"Close enough to embarrass me. Besides, what else does Mrs. Howard have to do? She can't get out of the house herself, so the next best is having people in. I hear they had a party for fifty the other evening." Junie didn't sounded embarrassed or regretful at not having been asked. "They love having you," she said, "so go and have a good time. Take them something from the freezer. Your father has some loverly stuff stashed away. Take the Sacher torte. No, better not. Much too fattening for Sandy. Take the—"

"Jem caught some mullet. They're all cleaned. We're taking those and some rye rolls."

"Perfect. Have fun, sweetie."

"Sure," Taylor said slowly. "You, too."

She hung up and stood for a moment, watching the ceiling fan revolve. Around and around. She studied the coromandel screen. It was beautiful. There was something funny, something very very odd about her mother lately. It wasn't just that she left the house nearly every day as soon as Tony had gone to work. Junie never had liked housework, as anyone could tell by looking around. It was more that she couldn't seem to stand the house itself anymore. She had always loved it.

When Grandmother Reddick visited, the place slowly got "put to rights."

Grandmother Reddick: You won't mind, will you, June, if I turn my hand to this and that while I'm here? You know I find it difficult to be idle.

Junie: By all means, Mother Reddick. Whatever pleases you.

It pleased Grandmother to polish furniture, re-arrange linen closets, take all the dishes and cooking things out and wash them and put them back in orderly ranks. It pleased her to mend and even to darn. Once she'd brought her own darning egg. B.J. had been enchanted, Junie had been astounded. It was her method to let rips and worn-out places in clothes or slipcovers remain as long as they were not too bad or too noticeable. Then, if stapling wouldn't do the job (they all had at least a few stapled-together shirts and pants) she threw whatever it was out. Junie did not shop in "stores." She had no interest in new things—new clothes, new slipcovers, new pots and pans. Taylor could not remember ever using a just-

bought bath towel, ever seeing a new skillet or coffee-
pot in their kitchen. Everything new that came into
their house was old, something some other family had
used and decided to get rid of at a tag sale. Or, of
course, at an estate sale, where the *good* old things
were found.

When Grandmother was visiting, Junie made an
effort. Not to be the daughter-in-law Tony's mother
would have wanted. That was beyond her capacity.
But she tried for and achieved (if the visit didn't last
too long) a well-meant sham. Beds got made in the
morning. Dishes were not left standing on the side-
board with bits of food stuck to them. They were put
in the dishwasher with bits of food stuck to them. She
presented herself in what she called "lady duds." Neat
slacks, skirts, flip-flops on her feet. Shirts over her
skimpy bikinis or maillots. What she could not do was
feel affection for her mother-in-law. But since the
attitude was reciprocal, since both understood that it
was Tony and the children they cared about, each
from her polarized position, they reached a sort of
accord. Provided the visits were not prolonged. Despite B.J.'s howls when she left, Grandmother Reddick had only once permitted this to happen.

When she did leave, Junie seemed to undergo a
feverish reaction.

The last time, when Tony had departed for the air-
port, B.J. sitting on Grandmother's lap and Drum

stretched in the back seat, Junie had thrown her shoes and shirt off the dock, tossed her arms in the air and shouted, "There she goes!"

She'd given a shout of laughter. "Look, kiddies! There's a cockroach! Do you realize, have you ever noticed, that we don't see a single *cucaracha* while she's here? Do you suppose they're *afraid* of her?"

Grandmother Reddick, in fact, employed a very powerful insecticide, pouring it into crevices all over the kitchen and the laundry room and the two bathrooms and her own room. She went to the market and got a bottle of the stuff if Tony had forgotten to get it in for her. It had a strong odor. It was impossible that Junie didn't know about this, and didn't know that Taylor and Jem knew, but nobody said anything as Junie whooped a welcome to the cockroach (even Grandmother Reddick didn't spray the dock), who certainly had timed his reappearance well.

"Look, you two," Junie had said. "I'm going over to the beach and run for about an hour. *I have to get some air—*"

She'd jumped in the skiff, released the mooring line and lowered the outboard into the water. "Thanks, luv," she said as Jem handed down the anchor. The motor started at the first pull and she went off too fast, leaving a wake where she was not supposed to leave one, out across the bay, under the bridge through the pass, and so around to the Gulf, where she would drop anchor near the beach and run for an hour or so. Junie was not tall and had a sylphlike body, but she was strong. Doing what she wanted to do, she was tireless.

That day, after watching her out of sight, Jem had jumped off the dock and rescued the shoes and shirt. He'd arranged them on a chair to dry. Taylor would have let them float away. But in neither case would Junie pay attention. Finding them on the chair, she'd be unsurprised. If they got carried off by the tide, she'd forget she'd had them.

Housework, marketing, cooking, cleaning up after cooking, seeing that people got to school on time, the dentist on time, looking at report cards, showing up on Parents' Night . . . all this exhausted Junie so that a tight whiteness seemed to appear under the rose-brown skin. She did most of those things, despite what Grandmother Reddick thought. But it seemed she was left emptied of spirit and energy by the effort. More so each year.

Now, in summer, with school out and no mother-in-law visit looming, Junie was winged. She never walked anywhere. She ran. She never sat still but darted like a lovely lizard in and out of the house in and out of the water in and out of their lives.

Taylor brushed her hair, got into an old one-piece bathing suit, put on a shirt of her mother's, went to the garage for her bicycle. As she pedaled through the village toward the Howards she let her mother slip out of her mind. As, no question of it, she and Jem and B.J. had slipped out of Junie's the moment she had hung up. And Tony, Taylor supposed. Though she wasn't sure of that.

~~four

The house where the Howards lived was surrounded by a high wooden fence with espaliered pyracantha growing against it. Junie said espaliering was against nature. "Just see," she'd say, "how that stuff wants to flourish, to send out streamers and branches in its own wild way, and there it is, *corseted* to that wall. Must be miles of it. Isn't it awful?"

The espaliered pyracantha was much admired in the village, and Taylor was among its admirers. She did not confide this to her mother, whose good opinion she valued. There were other things she did not tell Junie, for fear of encountering a look of kind amusement, or laughing disbelief. She had never, for instance, told anyone in her family that she'd like to go to Disney World, over in Orlando. At thirteen, she had pretty much got over the longing, but it had been strong in earlier years and she could remember crying nearly all one night because she had turned down an offer from Mr. Howard to take her with his family on a weekend outing. She didn't remember what excuse she had made. Not something that would make the Howards realize that her family laughed at people who went to Disney World. What had she said? No difference now. Jem had never been tempted by a trip to Orlando's fun spot. She'd asked him once if he wouldn't like to see it, and he'd just hooted. He'd thought she was trying to be funny. Jem didn't want to go anyplace, except out on the bay on his Sunfish. And, one day, out on the Gulf of Mexico with the catboat. The way some boys his age chafed to be old enough to drive, or just to get a minibike and run it on back roads, Jem yearned to be of an age to take *Loon* out on the Gulf on a broad reach and run before the wind, south to Boca Grande, and then tack back against a fearful headwind. Jem's heaven—a catboat. And, in time, a sloop. Big, but not so big that he couldn't handle it by himself. She had every reason to think that Jem would sail around the world before his twenty-first birthday. He said he was going to, and she believed him.

Taylor: Don't you want to take anybody with you?

Jem: You want to go?

Taylor: I might. I could see some pelagic birds. Stormy petrels. Albatrosses. Shearwaters. Oh my. Yes, I think I'd like to come along.

Jem: You're on.

Inside the fence with the espaliered pyracantha a long driveway led to Mr. Howard's big house. There was a broad sweep of lawn, green even now in summer. They wasted water keeping it that way, but waste never bothered Mr. Howard. The house had six bathrooms, a greenhouse, two swimming pools. One kiddy pool with a fountain, and a large pool with a diving board. Jem liked to come over here because he was such a good diver. He did not like chlorine and the water in the pool turned his tow-colored hair a very pale green (sort of the color of the green heron's egg), but three or four times a week he could be found here practicing his jackknifes and back flips and swan dives.

Mr. Howard owned some banks. Three, maybe four. He was a small round man, savagely devoted to his family. Several times a day, Taylor knew from

Sandy, Mr. Howard sat down in his president-and-chairman-of-the-board office in one or the other of his banks and telephoned home. He expected Mrs. Howard to be there and she always was. When he went on a trip, he took her with him. Whenever possible, he took his children too. Sandy and Dan still somewhat enjoyed it, although Sandy said she expected ingratitude to creep into her attitude very soon. Amanda was already ungrateful to a murderous point. Even seeing all those places, and going first class all the way, didn't always, said Sandy, come out to a lovely treat. They had to be with their parents every moment, trailing while their father read aloud from a guidebook. On the last trip, to Mexico it had been, Amanda had got restless and rebellious.

"For about fifteen minutes," Sandy had said. "Then he took measures."

"Measures?"

"To see that Amanda behaved herself."

Taylor did not know, nor ask, what the measures entailed. Round and brown and dumpling-dear as he looked, she would not want to be the daughter Mr. Howard was taking measures about. Or a daughter he wasn't, for that matter.

"Did you see the azure-browed mot-mot?" she asked without hope.

"Taylor, we were lucky to see the outside of the hotel. We were practically under house arrest, because of Amanda." She did not sound resentful.

Taylor parked her bike in a six-bike rack next to the four-car garage, walked around to the swimming pool area. B.J. was happily leaping and shrieking under the fountain of the kiddy pool. Taylor waved to him and went on to the big pool in time to see Jem climb the diving board and stride to the end of it. He poised there a moment, wriggling on his toes. Then, in a perfect jackknife, he slid into the water so smoothly that even the plastic water lilies floating on the surface rocked only slightly. Swimming the length of the pool underwater, Jem flowed out on the tiles at the other end and stood there shaking water from his greenish hair.

"Now, that's what I call a dive," said Mr. Howard, holding up his hands and applauding. "Keep that up, young fellow, and we'll have an Olympic gold medalist in the village." He glanced at his son. "Now, I just wish someone would ride up on a horse and show Dan here how to dive like that." Mr. Howard was always wishing someone would ride up on a horse and do something or other. No one, Sandy said, knew where he'd picked up the expression, but he used it a lot. "Well, well, let's see how you can do, hey, hey, Dan boy?" he went on vigorously.

Dan scratched his behind, walked slowly toward the diving board. In a way, he waddled. Doing it deliberately, Taylor thought. The Howard kids had ways of getting back at their doting, demanding, possessive, and—Taylor supposed—loving father. Mr. and Mrs. Howard were crazy about their children. Taylor, who sometimes felt disregarded by her own parents, wondered where the line ought to be drawn and if any family ever managed to draw it. There had to be some. Name one? The Dobkins. She was at their house pretty often and had never heard any fights. Never *felt* any fights. The way a person could, she was sure, feel old quarrels shimmering in the air of her own house. But you had that word *seems*. The Dobkins seemed to know where to draw that line between neglecting their many children and strangling them with attention. But *seem* was a word to be reckoned with.

She was not being fair to Junie and Tony. Nobody thirteen years old who was reasonably bright and had read a reasonable number of books, or even looked around her a reasonable number of times, could expect her parents not to have hang-ups. Hang-ups were not the exclusive property and torment of young people, even if plenty of young people thought that was just what they were and wouldn't admit their parents' right to anything, even to be alive in some cases. She didn't feel that way. She just wished her parents would calm down and grow up. She'd read a book once, a book on psychology of which she'd understood about every tenth word, but this much she'd got from it . . . some people never matured. These bodies grew up, grew old, but the inside beings went right on being kids. And it seemed that the older you got while remaining a child, the less able you were to cope. That was why the country was full of so-called adults drinking too much and taking drugs and eating too much. *Smoking.* Junie smoked. Taylor and Jem hated it, simply hated it, and she would not stop.

But Tony and Junie loved their children. It was hard for Taylor to believe that Mr. Howard could really love a son whom he now prodded this way onto a diving board.

"Come along, son," he was urging. "Show your friend here that you can dive as well as he can any old time."

Dan walked to the end of the diving board. "But I can't, you know," he said, and sprang into the air, trying for a swan dive. He landed on the surface of the pool with a *thud*, splashed down to the end in a powerful crawl, climbed out and looked at his father. "Told you."

"Ah, you don't fool me," said Mr. Howard with a laugh. "You bombed on purpose. Hi there, Taylor girl. We were hoping your beautiful mother would grace us with her company."

So he wasn't fooled? He knew his children tried to spite him and could laugh about it? Or pretend to laugh about it? Well, you didn't get to own three or four banks by being dumb, but if he recognized his kids' need to needle him, why did he needle them into needing to needle?

"Come along now, son," he was saying. "Let's see that again, and this time put your *heart* into it. Go on, Jem. You're on the board. Show Dan how it's done."

Jem did another jackknife. This time his legs tipped over. He's marvelous, Taylor thought. A ten-year-old marvelous kid. She glanced at Mr. Howard, who was looking gratified. Not so smart, after all?

Dan performed a sloppy jackknife, came up shooting water out of his mouth.

"Okay now, fella," said his father. "Guess we'd better get right down to the nitty-gritty. Go to the end of the board, son. Now, lean over, head between your arms, legs straight—"

Sandy's dangerous eyes sparkled. *"Right* face, *about* face, *present* arms, *drop* dead." She smiled at Taylor. "In a bit we can go to my room and play some tapes."

Mrs. Howard came out of the house, followed by a maid in uniform carrying a tray. A pitcher of iced tea, a pitcher of what Taylor imagined were martinis. Some cookies and little sandwiches.

"Drinkies, everybody," said Mrs. Howard as the maid set the tray on a table well away from the pool.

Amanda, who'd been lying in a rope hammock slung between two pine trees, idly pushing now and then with her foot and reading a magazine, got up and slouched toward the refreshment tray. She was not really a tall girl, but so much taller than the rest of her family that she'd developed poor posture. Trying to stay down with them, maybe, Taylor thought. Amanda was pretty, with a turned-down mouth and a listless walk. She did not look like the rest of the Howards, and if someone had ridden up on a horse heralding the news that she *was* not, after all, a member of the family, Amanda would not have crumpled under the announcement. She took a glass of iced tea and undulated back to her hammock without a word to anybody.

Mr. Howard, martini in one hand, a little cigar in the other, gold chain around his brown neck, looked at his eldest daughter thoughtfully, apparently decided she'd keep, and resumed hectoring his son. "Knees straight, fella, head well between your arms, now slowly forward—slowly, now—"

"Is your father a good diver?" Taylor asked Sandy.

"He couldn't fall into the water. No, what gets me is Dan. I can't decide if he's spineless as a sea cucumber, or operating on a level so different from the rest of us that he really doesn't mind being bullied."

Mrs. Howard tripped around to where the two girls were sitting. She was wearing a one-size-fits-all caftan that floated about her heavy little body, and downtown makeup even here beside her swimming pool. She always looked as if she'd just had her hair done.

She lowered herself to a lounge chair with a soft *ooof*, and smiled at Taylor. "My, how thin and pretty you are, Taylor. Quite the little undine. We were hoping your beautiful mother would grace us with her company."

Sandy looked away, smiling, and Taylor said, "She'll be sorry she missed it." She hadn't had a chance to say it to Mr. Howard. The kind of conversation you had with grown-ups like the Howards was pointless. Taylor's beautiful mother never graced them with her company. She never, not actually, got invited. To tea or to swim sometimes, except she never came. But not to affairs. Like the party they'd had here the other evening. Nobody had called the Reddick house and said, "We're having a little get-together for forty or fifty people and would just love to have you grace us with your company." Her parents wouldn't have come if asked, but they hadn't been.

Still, Mr. and Mrs. Howard said things that you had to answer as if they meant them since, after all, you were a guest even if your parents never were. *Why* were they never invited? Mr. and Mrs. Howard, maybe, didn't want to ask a cook to dinner, even if the cook was a chef? In that case, shouldn't she and Jem refuse to come here, too?

Mrs. Howard watched as her husband continued to instruct Dan in the fine art of diving.

"Sweet," she said comfortably. "Father and son. Lovely picture."

Taylor glanced at Sandy, who was looking at the sky, then at Mrs. Howard, who was dreamily drinking, looking softly content.

Maybe I've got it all wrong, she thought. Maybe Dan loves the attention. Jem and I wouldn't put up with it, only that doesn't mean Dan has to mind. Maybe it's relish to him. As she formed the thought, Dan ran down the diving board, kept running in air, pumping his legs wildly, landed feet first in the water, thrashed to the end of the pool, clambered out and turned to look at his father.

"Me Tarzan, you gasbag!" he shouted and ran around the house, disappearing behind some oleanders.

Mr. Howard purpled beneath his tan. Mrs. Howard, blinking rapidly, looked at her husband, glanced away, glanced back, started up, sank back, looked at Sandy, took a gulp of her martini and closed her eyes.

"Let's go up to my room," said Sandy.

"Okay." Taylor would have preferred to collect her brothers and leave. But Jem was calmly continuing to dive, not well, and B.J. was still splashing under the fountain while Viva ran round and round the kiddy pool, uttering her shrill bark.

They passed Amanda, still in her hammock. She did not look up. B.J. shouted, "Come and play in the kitty pool, Taylor! It's *fun!*"

"Kiddy pool, darling. Sandy and I are going up and listen to music. Jem is right over there at the big pool if you want him, okay?"

"Okay," B.J. said agreeably.

The Howard house regularly got put on the island house-and-garden tour in the spring. Taylor could see why. The grounds were so impressive, the inside of the house so big and expensive looking, with lots of ornaments and waste space.

Sandy's room was three times the size of Taylor's. Her bed, of cane and brass, had been bought in Italy. There was a huge Swiss wardrobe painted with Alpine scenes. The parquet floor was laid with fleecy Indian druggets, very handsome and unsuitable to the climate. The draperies were strings of beads that could be drawn back. At the side of the room opposite the bed part was a sitting area of huge cushions with low tables from Japan. All of this, it seemed to Taylor, came together in a wonderful fashion. If they ever had an estate sale at the Howards', she thought, Junie would really send us to the poorhouse. But how we'd go in style.

"Boy, that was something, wasn't it?" Sandy said, after she'd got a silky-raw voice twining around the sweet and bitter dreams of country love. "Maybe those spooky sessions with the shrink are doing Dan some good after all. I mean, it was my opinion that he thought letting Daddy beat up on him was part of the scenario."

"What'll happen, do you think? Your father looked sort of mad. Angry, I mean."

"Be interesting to see. My bet is Mother will be on the horn to Dr. Borden to find out how they're supposed to take this."

"Will he tell them? I thought psychiatrists just sat there and listened and everything sinks in and nothing comes out."

"Well, I'll tell you," Sandy said, scrunching down among the cushions. "I'll undertake to violate Dr. Borden's ethics. Dan hasn't said one single word to him, not since he started going there a year ago. What do you think of that?"

"It sounds crazy. What's the point of going if you don't ever say anything?"

"That's why I said the sessions were spooky. He goes, dummy, because he's driven there and dumped off every Saturday at eleven ayem. Except a couple of times when they couldn't find him."

"Did he make it this morning?"

Sandy nodded. "Just."

"How do you know he never says anything?"

"He told me. Could you keep something like that to yourself? Wouldn't you have to tell somebody if you'd been going to a shrink for a year and had only said howdy Doc the first day? He told me because he had to tell somebody."

"I wish you wouldn't call me dummy."

"Oh, hey . . . I'm sorry, Taylor. We get so we talk like that around this house, and I forget sometimes who I *am* talking to. We're a rude family, you know. Not *simple* rude. Impolite. Amanda can go days without uttering, and my father's a bulldozer. Mother treats the servants like servants, which is why we've had twenty-eight maids in seven years. Myself, I think it all comes back to him. He really is living in the wrong century. He wants to be king of the castle and only his wife will act like a flunkey, so he blows his top and Amanda goes under a stone and I don't care and the maids quit and now Dan turns on him like a tiger." She giggled. "Well, Dan isn't tigerish, exactly. But he certainly snapped, didn't he?"

A figure sloped past the open door. Amanda, headed for her room, one that Taylor had never seen and that was off bounds to the house-and-garden tourists. The day they came, Amanda locked herself inside and was not seen again until the tour was over.

Sandy shook her head as her sister went by. "All she wants, poor thing, is to do what the other kids do. She wants to be part of a gang but she never gets asked in. I don't know what it is about her. She seems to be the type that gets excluded on sight. Maybe because she's so mopey looking, only I don't think she'd look mopey if she could get *in* anywhere. She wants to hang around McDonald's picking up boys. Maybe smoke a joint now and then. Go to X-rated movies at the drive-in. Normal teenage yearnings wouldn't you say?"

"I hope not," Taylor said. She and Sandy would be going to high school in the fall and Taylor wasn't presupposing joy all the way. If Sandy's scenario was a forecast, it looked like being hell.

"Well, they seem normal desires to Amanda," Sandy said. "And she hates him for immuring her in his castle. One day Amanda's going to split and I'll be surprised if we even get a postcard from her for the rest of her life."

"Do you really think those are normal teenage yearnings? I mean, does everyone who goes to high school have to start wanting to smoke pot and look at blue movies? Here we are, Sandy, on a collision course with high school, and I don't think I'm ready, not *nearly*, for normal yearnings."

"Of course, there's the matter of those birds. That may hold you back. But I have to experience everything because of my career."

"Do you like Erica Jong?"

"Oh, sure. I mean, she's not such a hot writer, but she's so wild and uninhibited. If you read as much of this stuff as I do, you'd see that some of them—

modern female writers—stick in raunchy words like a person who hates raisins putting raisins in the cake because that's what she figures people eat, raisin cake. You know darn well she couldn't choke it down herself, but she cooks what sells. Old Erica now, she reeks like a skunk just naturally. What are you reading these days?"

"*The Adventure of Birds*, by Charlton Ogburn. Dumb title, but it's a marvelous marvelous book. I'm crazy about it."

"I'm crazy about you," said Sandy. "You just are the nicest person that ever lived. And I don't think you even try to be, that's what's so wonderful. Jem, too. Did you see how he let his diving go off a tad?"

Taylor nodded.

"There's class for you," Sandy said. She lifted her head and sniffed. "Hey, I guess Jem and Daddy have the barbecue started. Let's go. I'm starving. Aren't you?"

"I'm never starving. I'm never even hungry anymore."

"That's funny. You've always liked food. The sort that gets cooked at your house."

"Not lately. I mean, I'm not hungry lately. I have to eat or it would make them nervous, but I think I could just stop and not mind at all."

"Maybe you're sick."

62

"I don't think so. Oh well . . . probably I couldn't stop. I only feel that I could."

Across the wide hallway, Amanda's door seemed more solidly shut than the average closed door. Taylor thought it had a bolted appearance.

"Are you going to call her for supper?" she asked Sandy.

"Amanda doesn't eat with us since she became a vegetarian. She concocts fibrous green messes in the kitchen, and she's on a demand schedule."

That Amanda wouldn't eat with her family didn't surprise Taylor. Nothing that went on between parents and children surprised her, except when once in a while she ran across a situation where nothing seemed wrong. The Dobkins. As long as she'd known Chrissie Dobkin she'd never known her, or anyone in the large Dobkin clan, to be other than happy and cheery and loving and nice to everybody, even each other. It was unreal.

But she did find it odd that a vegetarian should want to hang around McDonald's. She said so to Sandy, who replied that it wasn't for the Big Macs, it was for the boys. "She wants to pick somebody up," Sandy explained. "I told you. She's ape over the notion of a boyfriend, except she can't get out of here to get one. McDonald's is kind of a singles bar for high school kids. I hear."

"Wouldn't she rather scout the health food stores? I mean, if she could? Boys at health food stores would be more her type, wouldn't they? Sort of weirdly wholesome."

"McDonald's or the Sprout Spout. Anything with a tassel will do for Amanda."

It took a moment for Taylor to understand this. *Too* much Erica Jong, she thought then. Sandy, in her way, had to be as much of a problem to her parents as Amanda and Dan.

Why did people have children? They—I mean, *we*, thought Taylor—sure aren't the joy and comfort reading *Little Women* would tempt a dreamer to believe. Thinking it over, of all the people she knew, *only* Chrissie Dobkin and her umpteen brothers and sisters were a joy to their parents. *Seemed* to be a joy. Even Jem didn't fill Junie and Tony with unceasing delight.

But it seemed to Taylor that if she had to put the blame somewhere, and of course she had to, then most of it went to grown-ups. Kids were born ready to love their parents, and most of them went on actually doing it. For a longer while, or a shorter while. She loved Junie and Tony, right? Most of the time. Right. Did Sandy and Amanda and Dan love theirs? Taylor didn't think so. Maybe in a way, once in a while. But Mr. and Mrs. Howard made it practically impossible.

Why did people have children?

She could remember once, ages ago, sitting on the dock with Junie and saying, "Chrissie Dobkin's mother is going to have another baby."

"Is she, poor soul."

"*I* want a baby."

"Then wait until you're old enough to have one."

"Junie, I mean I want *you* to have one. If Chrissie has a baby, then I want one, too. And *mothers* have the babies, not little girls."

"Not this mother, kiddo."

"But you had Jem and me."

"And wouldn't trade you for the world, but enough's enough."

"Okay, then I want a dog."

The next day they'd been down at the pound to get a darling puppy, who turned out to be Drum.

But a couple of years later, along had come B.J. Junie had been sick all the time she was pregnant, and Taylor wondered now if maybe the real quarrels between her parents had started then. Spats and tantrums had gone on before, but beginning with B.J. they'd got down to battling on a regular basis. Of course, they always made up. So far, they'd always made up. Would they always? How long did people go on saying horrible things to each other and then forget they'd said them? "That's unforgivable!" Junie had shouted at Tony this morning. Half an hour later, they'd been crying and kissing. How often could unforgivable things be forgiven?

She didn't know why people had children, and couldn't remember why she'd wanted a baby that time, except that Chrissie had been going to have one, which seemed a lousy reason. She wouldn't make the mistake now of judging by the Dobkin family and their freaky fondness for each other. You might not run across another family like that in your whole life. It was certainly too late to be part of one. Now that B.J. was here she could not imagine the world without him, but she sure wouldn't leap for joy if Junie sprung another one on them.

Down at the barbecue site Dan, driven by hunger, was apologizing to his father. Mr. Howard heard the apology out in silence, turned away without a word. Since he was not directly ordered to leave, Dan took it as a signal to remain, and he joined Jem, who was rolling mullet fillets in milk and cornmeal.

"Lemme help, huh?" he asked.

"Sure thing," Jem said to his friend.

Later, when they were biking home, B.J. riding with Jem, Taylor said, "Why do we go over there?"

"Because we like Sandy and Dan, I guess."

"I guess."

The house was dark when they parked their bikes in the garage. Jem switched a lamp on in the living room, turned on the fan above the dining room table and a floor fan on the porch. It moved its head from side to side like a spectator at a tennis match. After the air-conditioning at Sandy's, home felt muggily hot. In this house only Grandmother Reddick's room was air-conditioned. Sometimes they sat in there to cool off, but tonight they went right to bed.

Climbing to her room, Taylor wondered if what she felt was depression but decided probably she was just tired.

~~*five*

One Sunday morning Tony and his children were at the end of the dock, finishing breakfast. They'd had cantaloupe balls, chicken liver and bacon kebobs, crepes with strawberries and sour cream, and were at the café au lait stage for the children, black coffee for Tony.

Taylor, feeling her father's scrutiny, had managed some melon and a crepe. Thinking about those models who made themselves throw up, she decided she probably could without trying. She wondered if she'd ever really enjoy food again. Once she had loved eating and cooking both. Now she didn't like either.

But apparently she'd satisfied her father, because he

leaned back in his chair watching a school of porpoises on their way through the pass toward the Gulf of Mexico. Following a sailboat, porpoises could seem exuberant, leaping and speeding as if on a watery trampoline. But this morning there was a Sunday somnolence about everything. Out on a sandbar some pelicans and oyster catchers faced quietly into the gentle breeze. A few gulls went overhead, not pausing to beg. Benjamin, if it was Benjamin, stood on one leg in the water, seeming to look at his own reflection. The bells of St. Mary of the Sea could be heard faintly, sweetly, far away.

"Lookit the porpoises, Drum!" B.J. shouted. "See out there!"

"Honey, don't talk with your mouth full," Taylor said automatically.

B.J. frowned. "Don't you talk to me with my mouth full," he said.

Tony grinned. "Gotcha," he said to Taylor. He stretched his long muscular body, touched his mustache, yawned, smiled, stiffened as he looked toward the house. The children followed his glance.

There came Junie, speeding down the dock with an expression that shattered the calm air.

"All right," she said to her husband. "All right. What have you done with it?"

Tony's mouth tightened. "What did you expect

me to do with it, when I found out what it cost? It's on consignment at an antique shop, and don't ask me which one."

"Now, you listen to me, Tony Reddick. That was—that *is*—my screen. I bought it, I want it, I intend to have it, and you have no right to sneak it out when my back is turned—"

"I have every right, when you take nearly a thousand dollars out of the bank to buy a piece of junk like that when I'm having trouble paying the taxes."

"Do you realize, do you ever stop to think at all, what a humiliating, miserable, antediluvian, *filthy* position it puts me in, to have to share a checking account with you? Do you know what it does to me, having you know to the penny every damn penny I spend? Do you know what it makes me *feel* like?"

"I know what it makes me feel like, to have a check bounce. Do *you* know that I telephoned the light and power people and gave them hell for saying my check was no good and then I phoned the bank and found out my check *wasn't* any good? How's that for humiliating, antediluvian and all the rest of that crap? How about that, Junie?"

"There isn't one woman I know, not one other woman, who doesn't have her own checking account. Who do you think you are, to strap me into a position like this? I want an answer!"

Tony stood up. "You want an answer."

"That's what I said. And I'm warning you—I am going to get the screen back, even if I have to pay more than I paid for it in the first place."

"You've got a surprise coming, Junie. You don't even have a joint checking account anymore. I've started an account in my name, and from now on my salary goes into that, and you are going to learn to live on what I give you for household expenses—"

"Listen to me, you—you imbecile! I'm not your household helot, and I will not be doled out *household expenses*. You're crazy—"

"Who earns the money around here?"

"Earns? Earns! You mean who goes sashaying downtown to muck around with sauces every night? You call that *earning*? I am fed *fed* up with your mingy tacky ways. And I'm tired, *while* I'm at it, of Junie the cat threw up in the living room and Junie the bulb blew out in the bedroom and Junie we've run out of shaving cream and Junie the phone's ringing and Junie this and Junie that and Junie take *care* of everything. Earn? I'm the one who earns around here. And I'll tell you something else. I'm not going to *ask* you anymore if I can get a job, I'm going to get one. I will not listen anymore to what I spend and what I don't earn. No more, that's flat."

"Okay. But if you get a job, I'll quit mine. And if I quit mine, there is no way Jean-Jacques will take me back, and he'll certainly try to blackball me, and I'll end up somewhere on Route 41 frying things in deep fat. At a fifth what I'm making now."

Junie beat her fists on her head. "Oh . . . oh, you are so pig*headed*—" she screamed. "I'm like a mouse trying to work its way out of a maze and you're sitting up there in your white scientific smirk, cackling because there's no *way* out."

"That's not necessarily so. All I am set on is that the kids aren't coming home to an empty house. One of us is going to be here for them, and if it isn't you, it's going to be me. What sort of job do you fancy?"

"I *do* have a degree. Which is more than you have."

"Yup. A genuine B.A. in liberal arts. What do you plan to do with it? You can't even type."

"Type! If that isn't typical. Do you think that's all women are, typists?"

"I didn't say you are one, I said you aren't one. I'm trying to think of anything at all you could do that would begin to pay the bills around here."

"I could sell real estate."

"Oh, for God's sake, Junie. Everybody in Florida is trying to sell real estate to everybody else. You couldn't make walking-around money."

"You're going to be sorry for this, Tony. I mean it."

"Threats. Bills. Fights. I'm already sorry."

" 'Scuse me," said Jem. He leaned over the dock, gagging.

"Now, see what you've done!" Junie cried. "You're making your children sick!"

"Come on, B.J.," said Taylor.

"Come on where?" he whimpered.

"We'll go build a sand castle."

"I don't wanna build a sand castle!"

"We'll do something. Come *on*, will you?"

"Taylor," said her father. "Don't snap at him. He's upset. You'll just make him worse."

"So, so sweet. *So* understanding. Daddy will come to their defense when horrible Mommy makes a scene, is that it?"

"Somebody had better come to the defense of these kids. They're subject to what you rightly call horrible scenes all the time."

"How do you dare!" She pushed her fists against her face. "I suppose the scenes are *my* fault—"

"I'm damned if I think they're mine."

Jem got to his feet and walked down the dock without looking back. He went into the house, but whether to go to his room or through the back door to get his bicycle, Taylor couldn't guess. She picked B.J. up and carried him struggling in her arms toward the house. Behind her she heard Junie burst into tears, but like Jem she did not look back.

In the living room, she let B.J. slide to the floor. "Do you want to go to the beach, honey?"

"Why are they yelling that way?"

"I don't know."

"I don't like them to yell."

"No. Well, I guess maybe they don't like it either."

Why did they do it? Why couldn't they talk things out, quietly, reasonably, instead of going at each other like a couple of piranhas? Why, for that matter, shouldn't Junie get a job? B.J. could go to nursery school. As for us needing someone to come home to, she thought, that's a lot of bull. An empty house to come home to would be a garden of pure delight compared to what they had now.

Why didn't Tony trust her with her own money? Maybe if he did, she wouldn't buy coromandel screens and—all that other trash. Maybe she did what she did because he did what he did and if they both did things differently—what then? Well, things would be different, she concluded uncertainly.

Tony did pull that *Junie the cat threw up in the living room* thing all the time.

> *Junie: Why am I always the one who cleans up after the animals?*
>
> *Tony: You know it makes me sick.*
>
> *Junie: It doesn't whet my appetite.*
>
> *Tony: Well, I can't clean up after them and that's that.*

Or—

Tony: Junie, the phone's running over.

Junie: Funny. Funny. *Let it run over, see if
I care.*

*Tony: It won't be for me. It's probably
one of your madwomen from Antique Row.*

Meanwhile, unless Taylor or B.J. got it, the telephone would have gone silent. Jem would never answer it, unless requested, and B.J. could not be cured
of the habit of hanging up before he went to call
whoever was wanted.

"Taylor?"

"What?"

"Where's Jem?"

"I don't know, B.J. Maybe in his room. Go look."

As B.J. went in search of his brother, Taylor slumped
to the floor, leaning her head against the sofa. She
sighed deeply, pulling air into her lungs, holding it as
long as she could.

What was the matter with them? Did they hate
each other? No. No, they did not. When they weren't
quarreling, you could see how much they really loved
each other. Then how could they fight so much, say
such things?

Junie: Let me tell you something, Tony, in case it's escaped your notice . . . living with you is about as much fun as settling down in the old folks' home. In fact, when you and I get there, when we go hand in hand through those final portals, I am not going to know the difference.

Tony: I don't know what you're talking about.

Junie: Of course you don't know what I'm talking about. That's what I'm talking *about. Your idea of the fulfilled life is to travel within a thirty-mile radius of your house and get home before dark. When do we ever do anything, go anyplace, have any* fun?

Tony: What do you want to do, to have fun?

Junie: My God, anything would serve. I mean, I'd think I was in a whirl if I got to downtown Tampa. But since you ask, I'd like to go to New York.

Tony: New York City?

Junie: Yes. New York City."

Tony: Fun with the muggers and rapists?

Junie: Fun, you cretin, with theatres and museums and concerts in the park. They have concerts in the park up there, did you even know that?

Tony: I know it. When I go to a concert I don't want to have to be rescued from it. A person would be safer in Boston, and that's no safe harbor.

Junie: I do not want a safe harbor! I want to do something that's fun. I want to go someplace and hear some music and look at paintings, I want to go someplace and dance. Don't you understand?

Tony doesn't understand, Taylor thought. She guessed none of them really knew what Junie meant, because all the rest of them were happy to—what was it she'd said?—travel within a small radius and get home before dark. This place, this safe harbor, was what they loved. It was to live here that Tony had left Massachusetts. I'll go away some day, Taylor said to herself. A whole lot farther than downtown Tampa. But not to have the kind of fun Junie talks about.

She turned her head as her mother came in.

"Oh," said Junie. "That's you, Taylor." She came around the sofa and sat on the floor beside her daughter. After a while, she said, "I should apologize to you kids, shouldn't I? But then, I'd be apologizing all the time."

There was a silence before Taylor said hesitantly, "Are you awfully unhappy?"

Junie pushed her hair back. "Not really. I guess. Anyway, not all the time. It's just—oh, I can't explain. I never can explain so anyone will understand. Some people," she said in a low voice, "just shouldn't be mothers."

Taylor felt clammy. "You wish you didn't have us?"

"Darling, don't. Don't twist my words. Or my meaning, I guess I mean. Be the grown-up person you are. Of course I wouldn't be without you three . . . or without Tony," she added slowly, "for anything in the world. That's the truth. You know it is. It's just"—she shrugged—"I'm not a good mother."

"Yes. You are too."

"Well, that's wonderful of you. To say it, and maybe mean it. But we both know I fail all of you constantly."

"You're always telling me not to have self-pity. Be self-pitying," she corrected.

"Nice point." Junie reached across to the mother-of-pearl inlaid table, took a cigarette from a package, lit it, and blew out a long streamer of smoke. Taylor forced herself to sit still in the hated odor.

When several minutes had gone by and Junie hadn't spoken again, Taylor said, "Then why did you marry somebody and have kids, if you think you shouldn't have been a mother?"

"My Daddy," Junie began, "was the smartest man I ever knew—"

Taylor moved uncomfortably. Junie often said this, in front of Tony or anybody. Junie's father had been a Tampa lawyer who became a judge. Judge Bellamy. Taylor recalled him only faintly, and supposed he'd been all, or nearly all, that Junie, who adored his memory, claimed for him. Junie hardly ever mentioned her mother, but she spoke of her father as if he'd left the room for a moment and would be right back.

"—and Daddy used to say, *a person becomes what he's least afraid of being.* Taylor, I want to tell you something—lots and lots of women find that what they're least afraid of being is married and the mother of children. It seems such a normal, right, sanctified, unrisky course to take. The fact is, parenthood is the most dangerous profession of all. Riding high wires, or mucking around with knives in people's brains, or setting out to be a concert pianist—that's all a piece of cake compared with being a parent. The difference, you see, is that people who decide to be high wire artists or brain surgeons or great musicians set *standards* for themselves—"

"Grandmother says everyone should have standards."

"Taylor, I am not talking about lemon oil versus Pledge or lights out on school nights—"

Taylor didn't think that was all Grandmother Reddick had in mind either, but this wasn't the time to argue.

"I am speaking," Junie went on, "of the *art* a parent engages in. How many of us study that? I mean, study it as if it were quite as important as brain surgery or playing a concert at Carnegie Hall? It's a far far harder thing we do every day of our lives than those scientists and artists do. The job is practically impossible to do well, and it's the one most women elect to muddle through with no training at all rather than face what they call 'the world.'"

"Not so much anymore," said Taylor, interested in spite of what she was hearing, which seemed to be that even if she denied it, Junie now wished she had not become a wife and the mother of children. She'd chosen Tony, marriage, motherhood, because she had been afraid to try "the world," and now she was sorry. "Girls aren't panting after wedding rings the way they used to," she told her mother.

"In my opinion the number of young women who elect to hack it without some heavy biceps to lean on has been exaggerated. Even if they live with someone—or a lot of someones—beforehand, in the end most of them opt for marriage."

"And kids."

"Taylor, I am not going to be able to talk to you if you insist on taking everything personally."

Not fair, thought Taylor. Not fair! I thought that was what we were doing, talking about *us*.

"Are you aware," Junie was going on, "that women are the only enslaved group in the history of mankind that ever *voted* to retain its shackles, that had a chance to get out of the stocks but marched right back into them of its own free will? Who do you think has been defeating the E.R.A.?"

"What's that?"

"Oh, for heaven's sake, what do they *teach* you at that school? Needlework? The Equal Rights Amendment, Taylor. The amendment that would put women on a par, would attempt legally to put them on a par, with men. Although Daddy always said that enacting a law was one thing, getting people to abide by it quite another. Just the same, that bill is a chance. And who do you think is voting it down and out? Women, that's who. The women of the country are rising up and casting a resounding NAY."

"Why?"

"The damn fools think they might lose something they don't have anyway. The respect of men."

"Tony respects you."

"You will be subjective, won't you? You don't understand at all what I'm trying to say. I suppose I'm not making myself clear. Women, Taylor, are domestic animals. A man treats his cow well if he wants her to calve and give good milk. That does not mean he respects the cow. *Or* will let it have its own bank account." She frowned. "Listen, Taylor . . . in a few years you'll probably meet someone whose very touch makes you go up in flames. It's a glorious feeling. Nothing else in the world like it. If you're lucky, the flames last a long time. For some people, I guess, all their lives. Just the same . . . you can't live by flames alone and you'd do well to keep in mind that when a man marries, he gets a housekeeper. When a woman marries, she becomes one. And don't talk to me about those men who do the dinner dishes and hold her hand while the baby gets born. You could put *their* number in your grandmother's thimble." She lit another cigarette, having just put out the first. Watching the match curl and char in the ashtray, she muttered, "So much for flames."

Taylor stirred miserably. "You sound bitter to me." It was a word she had read but never used before. Bitter. A terrible word.

Junie got to her feet. "Sometimes," she said softly, "I feel as if I were living in a houseful of strangers. You are the only other female in the place, including those animals, and you're no more understanding than the males." She turned at the door. "If anybody asks, I'm taking *Merrywing* out for a while."

"Junie! Let me go with you!"

"No. I'd rather be alone."

After her mother had gone, Taylor looked down the dock to where Tony was slumped in a chair. He lifted his head as Junie dragged the Sunfish into the water, shoved off and ran up the sail. He didn't offer to help.

~~six

Time, which had taken them almost imperceptibly to midsummer, now took them past it in a rush, and Taylor got down to serious worrying about school. Until now, she'd liked it. But that was in the village, with teachers she'd known all her life. She wasn't a reader the way Sandy was a reader but found school-work easy and sort of fun. She could get there and back in fifteen minutes, riding her bike. She'd gone through grade school and junior high with scarcely a bump.

And now this. High school. School bus to the mainland. Huge classes. Strangers to learn from, sit with, be with, try to accomodate to. A vast new building, all glass and stainless steel, with two playing fields and an indoor Olympic swimming pool. The football team was the pride of the county. Soccer had been introduced.

"There was nothing the matter with the old school," she ranted at Tony when the two of them were out on the Gulf on *Loon* one morning. "Do you know they took down a slash pine that had an eagle's nest in it that the eagles had been coming back to for twenty years?"

"I'm sorry, Taylor. I really am. I thought eagles were protected."

"They're supposed to be. I don't think anything can be protected from *builders*."

"That's the worst thing you can call a person, isn't it? A builder."

"Tony! They're building over the murdered body of Florida! Everywhere, everywhere . . ." It made her ribs ache, her stomach ache, her heart ache, to think of the birds made homeless. Where did an eagle pair, an owl and his mate, go, who'd returned year after year to the same tree, when they returned and found a football field or a shopping mall in its place?

"Can't break your heart over that sort of thing," her father said. "Developers, destroyers—they're unstoppable. When I came to live on this island twenty years ago, it was still truly beautiful, and even then wasn't what it had been thirty years before that. And before the Spaniards landed, Florida must have been like the

Garden of Eden. Maybe that's what it was, and that's what we got driven out of, to make room for Miami Beach. As long as Homo Avaricious is around nothing much else stands a chance."

"It isn't just man, I guess," Taylor said reluctantly. "I mean—I watched a pair of green herons at the beginning of the summer, building their nest in the mangroves. They make a kind of ramshackle thing, you know. All herons do. But they take as much *pride* in it as if they were prairie warblers."

"Prairie warblers are good builders?"

"Tony, they make *beautiful* nests. Small, but marvelously constructed. Very deep, and closely woven, and lined with down. I'd live in one myself if I could. The way they attach them to the mangrove branches—it's hard to believe even when you see it."

"What about those herons?"

"Oh. Well, I went every day to watch. I hide in the shrubbery and look through my binocs. The two of them worked so hard. Then the female started sitting, and he'd bring her food and fuss around, and poke a twig here and there to be sure their crazy house wouldn't fall apart. And then she laid three eggs. Do you know what a green heron's egg looks like?"

"Mea culpa. No."

"Everybody doesn't have to watch birds. Actually, I'm glad everybody doesn't. I wouldn't want a crowd in there gaping at my herons. Anyway, the eggs are the palest sort of green. The color of Jem's hair when he's been swimming in all that chlorine over at Dan's. He hates it, but I love the color it gets. *Just* like a green heron's egg, really."

"I'd never have looked at it that way, but you're right. It's rather the shade of cream of avocado soup, from my point of view. Too much cream, I'd say." Taylor grinned. "Go on with your story," he said.

She sighed. "What happened—what I think happened—was that the great horned owl got the eggs. I went one morning, because I was going every morning, because I was so anxious to see the eggs hatch, and there was the whole thing—wrecked. The nest all pulled apart, the eggs gone. Owls do that, and there is one stops by there sometimes. You can tell when he's there because all the other birds make such a fuss."

"He has to live, too."

"I know that," Taylor wailed. "I adore great horned owls. I watched a couple of them, last winter, building *their* nest, except they don't really build one, they use an old osprey's nest and just add a little to make it seem like home. But oh, Tony—there isn't anything in the world more gorgeous than a great horned owl. Except maybe eagles. Or pelicans. Or practically any kind of hawk. Or warblers, of course. And there's the black-whiskered vireo—do you know that they're friendly? They kind of follow me around when I'm walking in the woods. I never can pick out my favorite bird."

"And isn't that great for you?"

"But those owls—they're very good parents. Most birds are, you know. Except cowbirds. Starlings, maybe, aren't so good, and I'd never trust a frigate bird. Baby great horned owls are the most adorable things you ever saw. They're the color of—if you took a cup of cream and swirled some coffee in it, that's the color. And they have these little tiny ears—they aren't either ears or horns, you know, just feathers. But they look like ears. Or horns. And big eyes that seem to look right at me when I watch them through the telescope. They'd lean against their mother, way up high in that nest—and that's in a slash pine too and I suppose it'll go down one of these days— Oh, I wanted to reach right out and *hold* one." She stopped, brooding. "Well, of *course* they have to eat, too. There's a theory, you know, that the reason the owls mate early is so that their babies will be hatched in time to rob other birds' nests. It's nature's plan. It's a shame we have to eat at all."

"If we didn't, I'd be out of a job."

"You'd find something else. Anyway, what I was saying—I guess man isn't the only destroyer."

"The difference being that creatures do it to survive

and men do it in order to spend money. I can't think of another reason, can you?"

"It's too bad money was ever invented."

"Most of the things that we've invented, or discovered, have worked to the general disadvantage of the planet. Get ready to jibe."

The boom swung over, the sail flapped, and for a few moments they were busy, Tony with the tiller and Taylor with the sheet. Then *Loon* was speeding with the wind now on her beam, trailing an arc of feathery whiteness, and Tony was staring thoughtfully at the telltale.

"What are you thinking about?" Taylor asked him at length.

"Trying to think of anything ever discovered or invented that did not have in it the potential, at least, for pain or destruction."

"Did you? Think of something?"

"Yup. The rubber spatula."

"Oh, Tony."

"I'm serious. It prevents waste, saves energy, and I can imagine no way in which it could be used to cause harm or inflict injury."

Taylor shook her head, smiling.

But later, when he'd gone to work, she wandered from room to room, her mind returning to the prospect before her. Four years of high school. She went into the room Jem shared with B.J. and sat staring at the aquarium. Tut followed, leaped to her lap, and the two of them studied the silent watery theatre. A yellowtail wrasse swam in and out of the rocks and weeds, passing and repassing a pair of baby groupers who stayed together like brother and sister, which maybe they were but who would ever know with a fish, including the fish. A tiny stone crab delicately fended off the wrasse with his lovely pincers. They had tips like black coral. A hermit crab in a moon shell skimmed across the bottom.

Taylor smoothed the cat's round silky head and sighed and wondered where Junie was. Where were Jem and B.J.? It was so quiet. The deep throb of Tut's purring. Frisky bubbling of the aerators in the tanks. Otherwise quiet, quiet. A cardinal singing . . . Her lids grew heavy, then closed.

When the telephone rang in the living room, Tut leaped from her lap and Taylor blinked dazedly. The phone stopped ringing as she reached it, started again as she turned away.

"Taylor? What are you doing? Why'd it take you so long to answer? I knew you were there."

Taylor yawned. "How?"

"B.J. and Jem have gone to the village for ice cream with Dan, and I figured if you weren't with them you'd be home if you weren't out with your mother, and you aren't out with her much anymore—"

"Was that you a second ago?"

"Of course it was me. What are you doing?"

"Nothing. I fell asleep looking at the fish."

"Could I come over? I mean, would you ask me to spend the night?"

"Sure, come on. Why are you whispering? I can hardly hear you."

"Taylor, I want you to call here and *ask* me to spend the night. So they won't think it was my idea."

"Gotcha."

Sandy hung up, Taylor dialed, got a maid, asked for Sandy. "Miss Howard?" she said. "Miss Taylor Reddick requests the pleasure of your company for this aft, this eve, and overnight if such is possible."

"Just a sec, Taylor. I'll ask my mother. Hang on."

With a strangling yawn, Taylor managed to wake herself up, and when Sandy came back with the news that her mother thought it would be a lovely idea, she was able to say alertly, "Come when you're ready, and let me say, Miss Howard, I am so glad I thought of it."

"Oh boy, me too," said Sandy.

In the kitchen Taylor found a note from Junie, saying she was playing tennis and would stay afterward for supper with the others of the doubles. Making four here for supper then, Taylor thought. Sandy was crazy about mushroom and onion quiche. Not exactly slimming, but you couldn't put a person on a diet on a visit if she wouldn't go on one when she stayed home. And maybe Sandy was right when she said people would have to love her for something more basic than a weedy bod. The fact was, most people were crazy about Sandy. Taylor thought maybe because she never moped. It was gladdening to be with somebody you could count on to be cheery when all about were losing their tempers or slumping into desponds. Tony said it was deeper than that. Tony said Sandy had a quality rare in anyone of any age— she'd caught on early that she was not the center of the universe. "Giving her an uncommon ability to see and hear other people. Most of us look inward most of the time, and can hardly persuade ourselves that other people actually exist." "Does that include me?" Taylor had asked, and hadn't figured out for ages why Tony had laughed.

Taylor sliced a sweet onion, put it in a skillet where she had butter just bubbling ("Onions cooked to glassiness for this dish, Taylor, never let them brown"). How she did enjoy her father's cooking sayings. *Meringues.* "They should be so light, so tender, that a breath will send them floating out of reach." *Rice.* "Pay no attention to the box instructions. Wash, wash, wash before cooking. Then boil in lots of water, like pasta. *No* salt." *Bread.* "You must see to it that your yeast is excited, but not to the point of hysteria." She cut lard and butter into flour for the crust.

Quiche, salad, iced tea, sherbet, some gingersnaps made by Jem. ("A commendable meal. You could serve it to the queen herself without a blush." "Which queen?" "Any queen. The queen of hearts. She might fancy a vin rosé to go with it.") Taylor did this often, carried on conversations with people who were not there. Could you call that talking to yourself? Especially if you didn't speak out loud? She'd ask Sandy sometime. What had all that whispering and scheming been *about*?

Well, there was one thing—if eating had lost much of its appeal, cooking had regained its. Rolling a pie-crust, grating cheese, stirring onion to glassiness, put her in a calm hypnotic state. She could see why her father liked his work.

When Sandy arrived with her tote bag, she sniffed the air and said, "Oh, you didn't! Oh, you did! Taylor Reddick, you've made a quiche for me! You just have to be the best friend a plump girl ever had!"

"That's as may be," said Taylor, using one of her grandmother's expressions. She set the timer and took it along while they went up to her aerie on the roof. Sandy took from her tote a nighty, toothbrush and toothpaste, hairbrush and a little bottle of pale pink nail polish.

"What's that for?" Taylor asked.

"I've decided to start painting my nails. Just the toes, to begin with, and this nowhere color. I'll work up to my fingers and magenta. You want to, too?"

"Okay. How do we do it?"

"Taylor, really. You just shake the bottle and take the little brush and go to it." Sandy sat on the floor, shook the bottle vigorously, wiped the brush free of excess polish and leaned forward. "*Ooof*," she said, straightening. "There is one real drawback to a bod like mine. Leaning over bends me out of shape. Now—let's see. Maybe it'd be better if I put my feet against the wall and sort of scrunched up to them." She planted her feet on the baseboard, wriggled forward, embellished her right big toe, sighed and leaned back on her hands. "How's that?"

"Super. But it's going to take time, if you plan to go in for this as a regular thing."

"Maybe I'll just begin with one toe. Do you think it would throw me off balance?"

"We could do each other's."

"Taylor, you dazzle me. Okay—you do me, and then I'll do you."

As Taylor applied polish to Sandy's plump pretty toes, rather liking the harsh aroma that rose around them, she said, "Are you going to tell me what all that whispering was about? I mean, I don't mind being in on the plot, but I like to be *in* on it, if you get my meaning."

"I wanted to get out of the house without having them think I was trying to escape—"

94

The timer bell went off.

"Wait here," said Taylor. "I have to turn the oven down. And don't spill nail polish on my Navajo rug."

"It's full of dog and cat hairs, and there're an awful lot of spots," Sandy called after her. "But I'll be careful, of course." When Taylor got back, she said, "Why I'm here is that all hell's broken loose over there and I wanted out and this was the only way I could think of."

"What's going on?"

"Well, Amanda came home yesterday with a new pair of pants and a new tee shirt." She paused expectantly.

"Okay," said Taylor. "I'm supposed to look dumfounded and say, 'But what's wrong with that?' This is a dumfounded look—" She leered. "But *Sandy*, what is wrong with Amanda's coming home with a new pair of pants and a new tee shirt?"

"The pants, Taylor, are so tight that she has to lie on the floor to zip them, and the tee shirt is yellow and has TRY ONE printed in lipstick red across the bazoo. No bra."

"Oh wow. Your father—"

"He's off the wall. I haven't finished. Are you ready for this?"

"I'm ready."

"Along with the new pants and the tee shirt, she also came home with a hickey on her neck."

When Taylor's expression remained blank, Sandy said carefully, "You don't know what a hickey is."

Taylor shook her head.

Giving her friend a long and thoughtful look, Sandy said, "You know, you're right. You aren't ready for high school. I don't think you're ready for the world at all. I think you should be put in a beautiful aviary surrounded by protective netting where you'd be safe with the other queer birds."

"Boy, do I ever think I'm not ready. It makes my stomach turn over, every time I think about high school. Are you nervous at all?"

"Sort of. I have nightmares about trigonometry, or being asked to spell Rensselaer."

"Why would you be asked to spell Rensselaer?"

"I don't know, I just get this feeling it might happen."

"Why don't you look it up and learn how?"

"I have, and I never can remember if it's two n's or two s's. I wouldn't want it to get out that I don't know how to spell. A novelist, after all. I mean, look at all the wonderful words I know and can use properly. But I can't spell them all. Once when I was a little girl I wrote a mystery story and I said the night was very eary. E-A-R-Y. The teacher wrote in the margin that of all the words in the English language, eerie most looks like what it's supposed to signify and that I was making my night something to laugh at, not shiver at. She was right, too. The trouble is, I don't think you can learn to spell well. I think it's something a person is born with. Maybe I'll have a secretary to take care of details."

"You didn't tell me what a hickey is."

"Oh, Taylor. Well, it's this sort of welt you get when somebody kisses you on the neck in a certain way."

"Somebody kissed Amanda? What certain way?"

"That I'm not sure of, and yes someone did. And a hickey cannot be brushed off as a wasp bite, which is what Amanda tried to say it was. My father took one look and hit the roof and went on through and when he came down he said Amanda was to be locked in her room on bread and water."

"You're kidding."

"Well, he wasn't. He said she wasn't to leave 'the grounds' unescorted for the rest of the summer, and meanwhile he is going to see about getting her into a private girls' school. The kind she'll board in." Amanda already went to a girls' day academy over on the mainland. "He didn't quite say detention center, but that's what he has in mind. Someplace really strict. He's had her locked in her room since last night."

"Bread and water?"

"Unless my mother smuggled some natural grain cereal up the back stairs."

"It's like a Victorian play."

"Isn't it? What beats me is what does he expect? She's sixteen. It's about time somebody kissed her."

"Who did?"

"Search me. Maybe she finally made it to McDonald's and connected. He and my mother thought she was baby-sitting at Dobkins'. He approves of our earning money. He says it will give us a conception of its value. For a banker, I don't know where he gets his conception of its value. What she earned all year baby-sitting Amanda would spend on a pair of shoes. I, for one, wouldn't baby-sit if it was my last hope this side of the tomb for getting a conception of the value of— What's that thing going off *again* for?"

"It's the second fifteen minutes of your quiche. Fifteen at 450 degrees, fifteen at 350. You want your quiche to be perfect or not?"

"Of course I want it to be perfect. I'll come down with you." She leaned over, grunted, put her finger delicately on the last painted toe. "I thought this stuff was supposed to dry fast. I'll just have to sit here, I suppose, until it does. When you come back, I'll do yours for you."

"Thanks. I've changed my mind."

When Jem and B.J. returned, Drum trotting behind them, they splashed into the bay to cool off, then dashed into the house shaking themselves, sand and water flying from them. Sandy, whose house was groomed like a Japanese garden, looked faintly disapproving. Probably, thought Taylor, if you've been brought up to think that things like rugs and furniture are almost holy objects then you can't help feeling that way even if you don't think that way. Sandy didn't worship an Aubusson carpet or a mahogany desk above comfort but she had an instinctively stern reaction when she saw how things were treated around here. Like Grandmother Reddick.

Grandmother Reddick: Tony, what's the point of June's buying a beautiful piece like that table, and I can imagine what it fetched even at an estate sale, if then it's covered to overflowing with ashtrays and magazines and dear only knows what else, to say nothing of glasses and mugs being left on it all the time. There are water *stains on it. And at least one cigarette burn. And that lovely Oriental runner in the hall. It's worn, but a fine thing, and there are shells and sand simply ground into it—*

Tony: Don't tell me. Tell Junie. She's the housekeeper around here.

Grandmother didn't try to hide her dismay, any more than she tried to disguise the odor of her insecticide, but she would not speak directly to Junie about water stains or sand in the rugs. She and Junie were firmly courteous to each other, and very distant.

Junie: Really, I have to admire her. It's plain she thinks her son and grandchildren are being sadly neglected, but there's never a peep out of her. Not to me, at any rate. What restraint!

Tony: Perhaps she'd afraid of how you'd react.

Junie: Oh, I don't think it's that. I wouldn't react at all, and she knows it. I think she's afraid of sounding like a mother-in-law. Poor things have been made the butt of so much cheap humor that they're intimidated.

Tony: I wonder what kind of mother-in-law you'll make?

Junie: I should think an ideal one, because I really won't care what's going on. Don't look at me as if I were heartless, Tony. Why would I care what grown-up people—and they'll be grown-up then, you must remember—do about their lives, or their children? Animals have these things better arranged. They hatch their eggs, wean their young, and then all parties concerned go their ways.

Imagine a bird lying awake nights wonder-ing how that one, the one who'd taken so long to crack the egg, was making out, out there in the trees on his little own. Imagine a mother cat brooding about that little six-toed tiger tom eight litters ago, he'd always been his own worst enemy—

Tony had laughed, but sort of sourly, Taylor thought.

Grandmother Reddick did not criticize, and Junie did not complain when the time for the next visit rolled around. Unless—"Here she comes, *radiating* pot roasts," Junie had said as Grandmother Reddick got off the plane last Christmas. Not unkind, really.

Once during each visit, Tony insisted that the family had to have a bouillabaisse dinner (fish heads left on) to sustain them through the pot-roasty meals they endured for Grandmother's sake. On that even-ing, his mother took supper on a tray in her room.

Well, she wasn't here now, nor liable to be for ages. Grandmother Reddick felt that only savages could survive a Florida summer.

After they'd eaten, Sandy and the three Reddick children looked at a horror movie. With Drum heavily asleep on the floor beside B.J., Tut asleep in Jem's lap, they sprawled in front of the television set, eating popcorn and watching placidly as limbs were dismembered, tongues torn out, as flaming bodies leaped from windows and splashed pulpily on the sidewalk, as a girl about Sandy's and Taylor's age was brutalized by a man from outer space who looked rather like a kangaroo. They saw it through to the end, turned off the telly without comment, and went to their beds to sleep peacefully. Only Taylor didn't quite turn off the day.

In the night, dreamily, she heard her mother's station wagon pull up beside the house and then, sometime later, her father's VW. She sighed and allowed herself to sink into dreams. She always, with some waking part of her, listened for the sound of their return and then, feeling safe, dropped, as it were, her mooring, and set sail for oblivion to the sound of bamboos creaking and sighing outside her window.

~~seven

When B.J., always the first up, came into the living room the next morning, he saw someone lying on the sofa. Curiously, he edged around to look, considered the sleeper for a while, and then, followed by Drum, climbed the stairs to his sister's room.

"Taylor," he said, shaking her arm. "Taylor."

She rolled around, sighed without opening her eyes, and said, "B.J. It's the middle of the night."

"No, it isn't. It's six o'clock."

"Boy, I wish I'd never taught you to tell time."

"Wake up your eyes."

"I don't want to wake up my eyes. Keep your voice down, B.J. You'll disturb Sandy. You want to swim, or have breakfast, or what? Why're you here?"

103

"I have to see your eyes to tell you. Wake up your eyes."

"Oh—oh, blast. All right." She blinked, yawned, stretched, yawned again, reached out and patted B.J.'s head and then Drum's. "What are you two doing here?" she said softly.

"Somebody's asleep in the living room."

Taylor stared. "Is this one of your stories?"

B.J. shook his head. "It's Amanda. There's a dandy longlegs crawling on her."

"Daddy longlegs. What's Amanda doing here?"

"I just told you. She's sleeping."

Taylor got out of bed, went over to Sandy and tapped her shoulder. "Sandy. Sandy, wake up. Amanda's downstairs asleep in the living room."

"I know."

"What do you mean, you know? Did you let her in?"

Sandy sat up. "I've been listening to the two of you. And who'd have to let anyone in your house? The doors are never locked. My father disapproves. Strongly. He makes me promise when I come over here to be sure you people lock the doors and get those things put on your windows that discourage burglars from crawling in."

"Really? You never told me."

"I don't have to tell you, I just have to tell him you will. Why he believes things I tell him is a matter for future colloquy. Do you know what a colloquy is? Most people think it just means a conversation—"

"Most people don't think it means anything."

"—actually it's much more formal than that. A colloquy is a discourse about something of moment."

"Then we should have a colloquy about your sister. She's supposed to be home locked up with bread and water and she's down in our living room asleep."

"You surely don't begrudge—"

"No, I don't begrudge. I think we ought to go down and see what's the matter."

"I guess we better. Those were delaying tactics. I don't, in actual point of fact, want to know what's the matter."

Taylor didn't blame her.

There was no sign of the daddy longlegs, but Amanda was certainly there. She stirred and sat up as Sandy, Taylor and Drum came into her improvised bedroom.

"Hi, kids," she said. "You look like a deputation. Or do I mean a delegation, Sandy?" She sounded nervous.

"How did you get out?" Sandy asked.

"The window."

"On knotted sheets?"

"Not necessary. I just opened the window and walked down the second floor porch and dropped to the garage roof and dropped to the ground. I hope the security at his banks is better."

Taylor looked at the new tee shirt with its lipstick red invitation, then at the pants. Amanda's legs looked like two snakes on the verge of shedding their skins. She stared at the hickey. You could have fooled her. It look just like the bite of a large insect. It did not look like something agreeable to get, but Sandy had told her the night before that high school kids valued them.

"I'd rather have a B-plus average," Taylor had said.

"Me, too. But there you are. Different strokes for different folks, as my father cares to say. I suppose they're like those dueling scars that German students used to flaunt. If they didn't actually get them by dueling, they'd inflict some on themselves. It made them look dashing. I don't imagine," she'd added, "you could inflict a hickey on your own neck, so I guess Amanda came by hers through the regular means."

Sandy certainly came by a lot of odd information, reading the way she did. Of course, she wouldn't know a prothonotary warbler if it nested on her headboard, but Taylor, who could read about the prothonotary warbler with tireless fascination, didn't think Sandy would have intense feelings about it.

"You could stop *peering* at me, Taylor," Amanda said fretfully.

"Sorry."

106

"I should thank you for letting me sleep here."

"That's okay. What's your father going to say? Won't he get even madder?"

"That is a matter of indifference to me, since I am merely waiting here until nine o'clock when things open downtown, and then I'm going to see my lawyer about a divorce."

Taylor's mouth dropped open. Even Sandy, who was hard to startle, let out a yelp. "Amanda, are you cuckoo? What are you talking about?"

Amanda turned to Taylor. "I am very very hungry, Taylor, and I just know there's something delish in your larder. *No* eggs or bacon or anything gross—"

"We don't have granola. You don't eat bean sprouts for breakfast, do you?"

"Not when I'm this hungry."

"Tony made brioche—"

"Eggs in it."

"French bread?"

"Marvelous."

While Amanda tidied up in Jem and B.J.'s untidy bathroom, Taylor assembled a breakfast of orange juice, French bread and mango jam for Amanda, bacon and scrambled eggs in addition for Sandy and B.J. She made hot chocolate.

She and Sandy carried trays to the table at the end of the dock and sat down. For a while nothing was said. They were not girls easily made wordless. But

Taylor sensed an uneasiness in Sandy that probably only Amanda could allay. *If* she allayed it. Was it a joke, some not funny joke, she was making? See a lawyer about a divorce? Had Amanda, oppressed by her father, the autocrat, finally freaked out?

"Does Amanda *have* a lawyer?" she asked finally, as they sat waiting for the runaway to join them. "Go ahead and eat or everything will be cold," she added, and sipped her orange juice.

"If she has, it's news to me. I thought only grownups and juvenile delinquents had lawyers. What all this is about a divorce—she's spaced out. There's no other answer. You can't get a divorce if you aren't married."

"Hey—maybe she is married. Maybe she got the hickey on her wedding night."

"Taylor, I don't think you're funny. This is my sister you're talking about."

"I wasn't being funny. People of sixteen can get married without parental consent. I think."

"Hoo. That'd put the cat among the pigeons."

B.J. had eaten and gone off with Drum by the time Amanda came strolling along the dock, blond hair smoothed, lips glossed, long legs moving sinuously in their ultratight sheathing. She looked pretty, defiant, and her shoulders were straight.

"Amanda," said Sandy, watching her sister drink juice, delicately spread jam on a piece of bread, sip her cup of chocolate, all in silence. "Amanda, are you going to let us in on anything?"

"Maybe."

"You *have* to explain."

"I don't have to do anything I don't want to."

"You sneak out of the house—"

"I did not sneak out. I escaped. There's a difference."

"Are you married?"

"Don't be silly. How could I be married? Who to? Jem or B.J.? They're the only boys I'm allowed to talk to."

"Which one gave you the hickey?"

"Don't be impertinent."

"What's this jazz about a divorce?"

"I intend to sue for a divorce from that family."

"Our family?"

"If you want to put it that way."

"What other way can I put it?"

"I intend to ask for alimony and child support."

"*Child* support!"

"I'm a minor, Sandy. That makes me a child, right? So I'm entitled to child support for being a child, and alimony for getting the divorce."

Taylor and Sandy regarded her with absorption. She could not be serious, but she sounded absolutely serious, and you had to admit it was some kooky marvelous idea.

"Who's your lawyer?" Taylor asked.

"Well, Daddy's. Mr. Swainson. I don't know any other lawyers."

Sandy snorted. "Amanda—do you know what's going to happen when you turn up on Mr. Swainson's doorstep with your petition?"

"What could happen that's worse than what happens to me all the time? The only thing he doesn't do is chain me to the wall."

"That'll come next. If you go through with this caper you'll end up on a cooky farm instead of in a girls' boarding school."

Amanda finished her chocolate, put the cup in the saucer and considered. "Well—then maybe I won't ask for a divorce. Maybe that's a bit extreme. What I'll do is—I'll have Mr. Swainson serve papers on him for disturbing my peace."

"Amanda!"

"But he does disturb my peace. All all all the time. I have no peace or freedom or anything of my own at all. And that's *actionable*!"

"I bet Mr. Swainson won't think so."

"Do you know what he said to me last night, when he was locking me in? He looked at me with that fat pink pouty expression he gets and said he *wished* somebody would ride up on a *horse* and tell him what to do with his *ungrateful* children."

"I have an idea," said Sandy. "Why don't we rent

a horse and hire a messenger. We'll have him ride up singing, 'Let Your Children Go!' I think a baritone, don't you?"

"Shut up. I wish somebody would ride up in a hearse and take him away."

"How *did* you get the hickey?"

Amanda looked at her sister, at Taylor, at the sky. "Oh, well. I met this fellow at the health food store, and—what are you two gaping about?"

"Nothing. Well, something. I mean, one day Taylor and I were talking about you—affectionately, mind—and saying how you should really be allowed to have a boyfriend and I said I thought you'd like to hang around McDonald's like the other kids and Taylor said she thought you'd find people more—congenial—in a health food store. That's all."

"What a bright girl you are, Taylor," Amanda said. "That's just how it happened."

"When?" Sandy asked. "I wouldn't have thought you'd have an opportunity."

"After all, nobody stops me from going for my raw nuts and sun-dried unsulphured fruits."

"Somebody'll stop you from now on. He'll hire a Pinkerton, round the clock."

"No, he won't. If lawyers won't do anything for me, I'll run away. I'll become a child prostitute in New Orleans."

"You're too old," said Sandy. "I understand they range from eight to twelve. If you're sixteen, forget it."

"Who's the boy?" Taylor asked. "Is he from around here?"

"Oh, no. He's from California, but his family just moved here. They bought a house way down the island."

"When did you meet him?" Sandy asked.

"Yesterday. After I'd bought my new outfit in a boutique next to the Sprout Spout."

"Yesterday. And a hickey already. Gosh."

"What's his name?" Taylor asked.

"Alexander."

"Alexander what?"

"We didn't exchange last names. We want to meet on a plane only of essentials. Besides, even if he just moved here, he might recognize Daddy's banks from his name being plastered all over them. I don't see why he can't be the Fifth National or something, instead of Howard Bank and Trust. It's ostentatious."

"How does somebody give you a hickey?" Taylor burst out.

Amanda rose. "You go too far. I'm willing to talk things over with the two of you, because I sense your basic sympathy. But some things are sacred."

"Sorry," said Taylor. "I didn't mean to be rude."

Amanda, who'd been talking so far in a light and

lofty tone, sat down again. She put her hand across her mouth in a forlorn, grown-up gesture. Tears dangled in her lashes but she did not cry, merely sat there blinking. After a while she said, "Do you ever get sick of yourself? I mean, this your *self*, this body you have to stay in and push around from place to place and put up with its moods and get sick with it if it wants to get sick and *feel* what it wants to feel— in your head or your heart or whatever the stupid thing wants. To the end of your *life* you're stuck with it. I can't stand being inside this *myself*. I want to get *out*." She looked at them tiredly. "Oh, what's the use of talking to kids?"

"Amanda," said Sandy. "You know what I think?"

"What?"

"I think instead of going to Mr. Swainson, you should go to see Dr. Borden. I mean, don't ask him or anybody, just go to his office today and sit there until he sees you. I mean, even if Dan doesn't ever talk to him, he keeps going back, doesn't he? So there must be something Dr. Borden does, or—or *projects*, while they sit there not talking that does something for Dan. Wouldn't you say?" she pleaded.

Amanda picked up a spoon, turned it around, put it back on the table, got to her feet again. "Okay, Sandy. All right. That's what I'll do. I have to do something. . . ."

She walked down the dock, shoulders slumped in the

old manner. They heard her car start up and go slowly out of the driveway.

Sandy exhaled a long sighing breath. "Oh, gosh. It's awful. Do you ever get sick of your *self*, Taylor?"

"I never thought about it until this minute. I mean, it's what I've got, this myself. It's who I am. I don't know what I'd do if I couldn't stand being inside it. Except you're right. I'd go to a doctor, not a lawyer."

"Oh, she was just making noises. She never intended to go to Mr. Swainson."

"Do you think she'll go to Dr. Borden?"

"I hope so. If she doesn't, I'm going to talk to my mother. Of course, she'd just go fluttering to *him*. I don't think she's had a whole entire thought of her own since she met him."

"Then what happens to Amanda?"

"I think I'll call Dr. Borden myself. I mean, if Amanda doesn't go there today. I wonder who this Alexander is."

"A fast worker, anyway."

"Some crazy from California. Gives me the creeps— it's crawly, the whole scene."

"Do you get sick of your *self*?" Taylor asked.

Sandy jumped to her feet and started to clear the table. "I most certainly do not," she said loudly. "In fact, I can't get enough of myself, and that's a fact."

"Do you suppose that Mr. Swainson, that lawyer, is related to William Swainson?"

"Maybe he is William Swainson. I don't know his first name."

"Sandy. William Swainson—the famous English naturalist. He had three birds named after him. Swainson's thrush, Swainson's warbler, and Swainson's hawk."

"How do you get even one bird named after you?"

"Same way you get a flower, or a disease. You discover it."

"When did this fellow live?"

"Nineteenth century. I think. Maybe eighteenth, but probably nineteenth."

"Something fishy about it."

"Why do you say that?" Taylor asked irritably.

"One man discovering three new birds. Could you discover three new birds, for all the looking you do?"

"Wouldn't it be nice? I'd like to identify a new hawk. Or a bittern. Did you ever see a least bittern? They're adorable, Sandy, simply adorable. *Reddick's bittern.*" She sighed, smiled. "And he could find three new ones because he lived when they hadn't got everything tabulated and computed and cross-hatched."

"Cross-referenced, you mean."

"I mean when there was still something left to discover. Now they spend their time identifying what's dying out, not what's coming to light."

"If I had a hobby that regularly made my spirits rainy, the way birds do yours, I'd find something else to be fascinated by. Something cheerier."

"Like what? Needlework?"

"You can be sure the running cross-stitch will never fall victim to pesticides, the way your birds are doing."

Neither of them was sure that there was such a thing as a running cross-stitch, but neither had any intention of becoming a needlewoman. Sandy would continue to read and keep her journal and dream toward the day when she'd see her name on the spine of a printed book. Taylor, willy-nilly, would rise at dawn and go out with her binoculars to spy upon nests, search the sky, delight in the sight of familiar birds and long for a glimpse of one she'd never seen before.

It occurred to Taylor that Amanda would benefit from what Sandy called a "hobby" and she herself privately thought of as a passion. But no matter what you called it—a passion, a hobby, the pursuit of a dream—it came out to caring terribly about something besides yourself, and Amanda could use some of that.

~eight

After the coromandel screen incident and the closing of their joint bank account, Junie stopped going to sales. She never, that Taylor or Jem knew of, mentioned the screen again, but one day, in humble accents, she asked Tony if she could have ten dollars a week to take yoga lessons with Mrs. Danziger and some other women.

"It's ten dollars a session, but I would only take one a week. I mean, if you'll let me have one, and then the rest of the time I can practice by myself. Bette says I can borrow her book, and look at that, so I wouldn't have to pay for it."

"You're a punisher, aren't you?" said Tony.

"I can't think what you mean by that. If you think the ten dollars is too much, maybe I could just watch the others, and try to copy, without paying for the teacher. They're all taking three lessons a week, but I explained to Bette that of course that was out of the question for me."

"Oh, boy. Look, cut the pitiful-Pearl pose, will you? The kids will think I'm Simon Legree."

"The kids don't know who Simon Legree is. Was."

"I do," said Taylor. "He was the villain in *Uncle Tom's Cabin.*"

"Do you people read that?" Junie asked, surprised.

"Not us people. Sandy. She was telling me about it, so I read it."

"What did you think of it?"

"I hated it."

"Then why did you read it?"

"Because I'd started."

"Taylor, you don't always have to finish what you start. By no *means* do you always have to finish what you start."

Taylor, realizing unhappily that Junie wasn't talking to her, didn't answer.

"Junie," Tony said, sounding desperate. "Look, Junie—"

"Look at what?"

"At me, for starters."

"So—I'm looking at you. Do you realize that in

some lights your eyes look yellowish? And sort of opaque. Interesting."

"Look, Junie—"

"Again?"

"I can't put up with this anymore."

"Up with what?"

"This silent treatment I've been getting. We'll open the bank account in both our names again, and you can spend what you want, buy what you want. I don't know, maybe it's a disease and you can't help it."

"Well, the cure certainly worked. If I don't have any money I can't spend it, can I? Short of borrowing from somebody, and I'd starve to death before I'd borrow from anyone, including you."

"Will you stop dramatizing! You aren't going to starve to death and I just said we'll open the bank account, so please—let's have an end to this. It's got me to the point where I can't work. I overseasoned the vichyssoise last night, and broke a platter. The soup was almost inedible and we had complaints."

"Oh, tut."

"I have to go feed my fish," said Jem. Taylor followed him into his room and watched while he dropped a few pieces of minced scamp into the water. The groupers and the wrasse rose to the surface for their share, but the two crabs, the hermit and the stone, waited quietly on the bottom as dinner drifted down.

"What happened to the sargassum fish?" Taylor asked.

"He didn't take to captivity. I made everything as nice as possible for him, and safe, and he got meaner by the day. He ate my sea trout. So I let him go. Maybe by now something's eaten him, the dope."

"I guess he didn't want to be safe."

"Guess not."

After that, Junie went nearly every day for yoga practice at Mrs. Danziger's, although the guru, or whoever taught them, came only three times a week. At home, Junie could be found standing on her head—from which position she was quite able to carry on a conversation—or sitting with her legs folded, palms resting together in front of her, eyes closed. When she was in that position it came to be understood that no one was to address her at all, much less try to have a conversation or get or give information.

Taylor: I'm supposed to go to the dentist, Jem, and Junie's out there meditating. Should I tell her?

Jem: Sure.

Taylor: Easy for you to say. Once I tried talking to her when she was lotussing and communing and I don't think she heard me.

*I mean, I looked right at her eyelids and they
didn't move the tiniest bit.*

Jem: Then don't tell her.

*Taylor: What about my dentist appoint-
ment?*

Jem: Take your bike.

Taylor: It's too late now.

*Jem: Call them up and say the car's broken
down or something. Otherwise they'll
charge.*

The yardman, who came once a month, came when
Junie was in a trance. After some debate with herself,
Taylor told him just to rake.

*Tony: Didn't Parrish come today? I mean,
the place is raked but nothing else. Did he
get called away early? The guy's left a bill
for an afternoon's work and all I can see is a
touch of rakage.*

*Taylor: I told him just to rake. I mean, I
didn't know what else to tell him.*

*Tony: I wanted that reclinata trimmed,
dammit. Where was your mother? Why
didn't you ask her?*

Taylor: She was in the lotus position.

Tony: Oh, for—oh, my God—

It had fallen from his lips in a sort of real prayer,
that *oh, my God!* Taylor, hearing it, felt brushed by
uneasiness. Something more than uneasiness that she
would not call fear. She had never been fearful. Had
she? There was a family story to the effect that when
she'd been very small she'd been afraid of rain falling
on her head. Junie said it was because some visiting
cousin had turned the hose on her, using the spray
nozzle, when she hadn't expected it. The story went
that she'd run up to her parents' bedroom and crawled
under their big double bed, the way Drum did now
when storms threatened. There was no getting Drum
to emerge until the last of the thunder had trundled
off to Mexico or the Caribbean, but they said that
she had been lured out that day by a dish of strawberries with sour cream and brown sugar. Tony had
put it on the floor where she could see it but had to
crawl out to get it. How old had she been? A year
and a half, around that, they said, no one actually
quite remembering. Taylor could not recall being
afraid of the rain, and she still loved strawberries with
sour cream and brown sugar. What she felt now had
nothing to do with that sort of fear. Or—maybe it
did. Maybe she was feeling the way Drum did when

something he couldn't understand troubled the air.

Tony and Junie didn't yell at each other anymore. That should have made things less threatening. Why didn't it? Because, probably, they seemed to have things arranged so that they were hardly ever together. Tony left for work after lunch and didn't get home before midnight. By then Junie would have gone to bed. Taylor, who went to bed whenever she felt like it, would look at her parents' door on her way upstairs. There was never a light shining around the cracks after 11:30. Tony usually slept until about nine, and by then Junie would be gone. To the beach, to play tennis, to her yoga sessions. When she got back, sometimes for lunch, sometimes not, Tony could be anywhere—out fishing or sailing with one or two or three of his kids. At the beach. In his workshop in the garage. He could be at the end of the dock, reading, and might glance up when Junie drove in. But he didn't put his book down and walk to meet her halfway, as she went halfway to him and into his arms, as it had been in the old days. When had the old days stopped? Were they going to come back, or was everything going to stay like this—silent and polite with the two of them, both of them being extra bright and careful with their children? And who got fooled by that? Not us, thought Taylor. B.J., usually so bouncy and biddable, had taken to *sidling*. He eyed his parents, whichever he happened to be with, until they turned their heads away. He resisted their suggestions for entertainment.

> *Tony: Come on, B.J., I'll teach you how to play poker.*
>
> *B.J.: No.*
>
> *Tony: Ah, come on. Draw, stud—you name it.*
>
> *B.J.: No.*
>
> *Tony: Okay, then. Let's go out on the jungle gym and make like monkeys.*
>
> *B.J.: I don't want to.*
>
> *Tony: Trampoline?*
>
> *B.J.: No.*

It wasn't always like that, but it was often like that.

Taylor and Jem didn't discuss the situation. Taylor suspected that was because they were afraid talking about it would *make* it a situation. Yet it was one, whether they talked or not.

Jem kept his own counsel, Taylor was sure. He'd always been pretty open with his family, but she could not picture him going to Dan, or any of his other many friends, and being open about the family to them.

She herself was not immune to the idea of being able to talk to somebody. She had almost decided to consult levelheaded Sandy when something Sandy said changed her mind.

Taylor had fixed a picnic and the two of them paddled the canoe over to Wrasse Island. Drum, who would certainly have been a sailor had he been a man, pleaded to go along. He'd barked happily when the girls began pulling the canoe into the water, and had waded in after them with an air of confidence, as if there could be no question of his coming along.

Taylor had turned and said sternly, "No. Stay."

Drum, pretending not to hear, pranced in the shallows, ducked down, front legs spread, rump up, tail wagging. Then he straightened and headed for them again.

"No, Drum! You are not coming. *Stay*, I said."

He shook his head, gave a little leap, sat down in the water with his head on one side. *You can't mean it*, his eyes said.

"I do mean it," Taylor replied.

But that's cruelty to animals!

"It is not," said Taylor. "I want to look at birds and you scare everything with your barking and racing around."

*I can't help it. I feel so good, riding in the boat,
running around the island.*

"I know you can't help it, and you can't come,
either."

This exchange took place, naturally, in silence, and
as they paddled off, Taylor in the stern, she had to
force down a feeling of guilt and betrayal.

"He gets to sail practically every day," she explained to Sandy. "Sometimes more than once."

"Who?"

"Drum, of course."

"Taylor. Are you feeling guilty about the dog?"

"I guess."

"How dumb can you get? By now he's forgotten all
about us."

They turned, to see Drum swimming after them,
his dark head sleek and seallike, his purpose steady.

"Ah, gee," said Taylor. "Look at that."

"Why can't he come with us?"

"He scares the birds."

"Then you are at a crossroads. Where does your
loyalty lie? To your dog or to the birds of the air?"

"Let's wait for him."

They back-paddled until Drum caught up, then
clutched his slippery clambering body to help him in.
Once aboard, he shook water from his coat so vigorously that he lost his footing and sprawled on the bottom.

126

"Will you for Pete's sake sit still!" Taylor snapped, and caught Sandy's puzzled glance. "Why are you looking at me that way?"

Sandy shrugged.

"No, I want to know."

"You seem a bit jumpy lately, that's all. I think he's pretty cute, coming after us that way. Besides, if you keep talking to him in that tone of voice, he wouldn't dare bark at a falling leaf, much less one of your precious birds."

Drum, indeed, was lying down, looking subdued. Usually he stood in a boat, head up, mouth open as if in delight.

They paddled on, Taylor biting one side of her lip and then the other. Her precious birds, Sandy said, with a sort of kindly scorn. As if she put birds in front of other loyalties. Suppose, she asked herself, you had to choose between keeping Drum and seeing a scissor-tailed flycatcher? She'd never seen a scissor-tailed flycatcher and she longed to, in the true sense of the word. She longed, yearned, desired, desperately wanted to see, with her own eyes, the scissor-tailed flycatcher. But if to see one meant giving up Drum, she wouldn't hesitate. She'd choose to keep him.

Sandy didn't understand. In fact, Taylor knew no one else who shared with her the maybe odd, but certainly heady and always thrilling, bewitchment of birds. It would be wonderful to share it with somebody, but so far no one had turned up. Taylor belonged to the Florida Audubon Society, and had once gone to a meeting. There'd been no other kids there, and the adults had gathered around her as if she were a rare sighting, clucking and smiling and explaining and exclaiming until she thought she understood the sensations that Ross's gull must have had when he landed from Siberia on a beach in New Jersey. Birders from all over the world had dropped whatever they were doing and headed for the Jersey shore, wanting a glimpse of the rare exotic. Taylor could imagine him sitting there, lonely and confused, far far from home, looking around the beach for something to eat, while thousands of binoculared and telescoped human beings watched his every move. She had not gone to a second meeting although two or three people, sounding very nice, had telephoned asking her to.

At Wrasse Island, she and Sandy pulled the canoe ashore. Drum's chastening proved temporary, as Taylor had known it would. He hurtled down the beach, scattering sand, came scampering back, legs flying to either side. Suspecting danger, he went yelping into the woods, came out farther down the beach and stood barking to sound the all clear. Taylor, who had her binoculars with her, since she never left the house without them, put them back in the case, put the case in the picnic hamper.

"I get your point," said Sandy.

"Oh, well. He's having fun." There was a barred owl on Wrasse Island, and Taylor had been hoping to see him. Hopeless now. But you couldn't help being happy with Drum. Six years old and behaving like a puppy.

The two girls walked slowly to their favorite picnicking spot, put the hamper down and poked around for a while on the beach, finding a couple of nice pieces of driftwood. They swam, dried off in the sun, and then Sandy said, "*Please*, Taylor. I can't wait another second to see what goodies you concocted for us."

Smoked mullet salad, bread & butter pickles, cheese wafers, two mangoes at the perfect pitch of ripeness.

"Oh, Taylor," Sandy moaned. "Let me at it."

Somehow here on the island, away from home, Taylor found that she, too, was hungry for the picnic.

When they were peeling their mangoes, letting the juice run down their wrists, their arms, because they could go in the water and rinse it off, Sandy said, "Look at this thing, Taylor." She held the mango out. "Just look at that color. Like a winter sunset."

"Winter sunsets are more the color of tomato soup."

"They're the color of mangoes. And have you ever tasted anything, I mean *anything*, more sublime than a mango of just the proper ripeness?"

Taylor shook her head and chewed with her eyes

closed. Tony said food tasted better that way. She didn't find it to be so. She opened them, smiled contentedly at Sandy, at Drum, who'd had to make do with a couple of cheese wafers since he'd come to the picnic uninvited.

They threw the mango pits and peels into the woods, went into the water and splashed around, came back on the sand and packed the remains of the picnic in the hamper. Then they sat silent for a while, looking across the water from this little island to the big island where they lived. Drum, exhausted from hilarity, lay on his side in the shade.

Taylor was considering some way of unburdening her burdened spirits without being disloyal to her parents, when Sandy spoke.

"Amanda told Daddy she's going to go to Dr. Borden or run away or kill herself."

"Then she went to see him that day? Dr. Borden?"

"Yes, isn't that funny? She did just what I said she should do. Went down to his office and sat there until he came out, I guess with some other patient, and told him she *had* to see him. So he saw her, on his lunch hour. He must be a pretty okay guy."

"What did they talk about?"

"She didn't tell me anything else. Just stopped by my room that night before she went to bed and said the above. That's all. Oh, she said thanks."

Taylor could imagine Amanda, in her tight tight

pants and her braless invitational tee shirt, facing down some receptionist who was trying to tell her she could have an appointment the week after Christmas. Amanda smoldered. She could smolder lying in a hammock drinking iced tea on a summer afternoon and be somehow menacing. Taylor pictured the receptionist. Middle-aged, thick-waisted, totally at a disadvantage with a sexy teenager, trying to look scathing, succeeding only in looking crabbed with envy.

"Young woman, you can't wait here."

"Oh, can't I?"

"Doctor is exceedingly busy today. Much too busy to see you even for a moment."

"He'll see me."

Taylor could imagine such a scenario easily, and concede that it might be altogether wrong. Maybe the receptionist had been sexy-looking and Amanda piteous. What she couldn't dream up was the scene in the doctor's office. Would there have been tears, threats, obscenities, entreaties, defiance? Anyway, not silence. No psychiatrist would be able to tolerate two members of the same family filling their fifty minutes with silence.

"What did your father say?"

"That she can go. To Dr. Borden, I mean. I think she scared him. You can't be sure she wouldn't run away, or even kill herself. People do."

131

"I hope he helps her."

"So do I," said Sandy, sounding detached. "Of course, who should be going to him is the two of them. But that's a cliché, isn't it? It isn't the kids should be at the shrink but the parents who drove them to it."

"Do you get along with your parents?" Taylor blurted. "I mean, you always seem to, but do you?"

"Sure. I get along with them because they aren't important enough to me not to get along with. I guess Amanda and Dan are still looking for something from them, so that's why they act like such a pair of idiots."

"What do you mean?"

"I mean kids—most kids—expect all sorts of things from their parents, just because they are their parents. They expect them to be large-spirited and wise and loving and reassuring and all that garbage. Whatever kids are supposed to be hungry for."

"Aren't you hungry for those things?" Taylor asked, bewildered. I certainly am, she thought.

"Not the way I'm hungry for mangoes or smoked mullet salad."

"Sandy!"

"You think I'm kidding? I found out long ago that they aren't able to be large-spirited or wise or etc., etc. Not their fault, I suppose. But I don't care. They could both drop through a hole in the floor and I wouldn't know they were gone or remember they'd been there."

"That's terrible! That's a terrible, awful thing to say."

"Look, Taylor. You ask me something and I give you an honest answer and you freak out. I didn't say I *wanted* them to drop through a hole in the floor. They can go on living, for all of me. I just said they aren't important to me, and they aren't. I'm important to me, books are important to me, you're important to me. I like Amanda and Dan very much. I like them a lot better since they started standing up for themselves."

"Do you ever stand up to your father?"

"You just don't get the point. I don't stand up to something I don't even consider is there. When the time in my life comes for some upstanding, I'll do it, don't worry. But until then, forget it. I can't waste my time."

"Don't you think you're sort of taking—taking all sorts of things under false pretenses?"

"What things? What pretenses?"

"Well, Sandy. A lovely home, for one."

"You sound like a two-year-old. What should I do? Run off and be a child prostitute in New Orleans? I admit I'm the right age, but I don't have tastes that way. I'm thirteen and have a way to go before I can be on my own. Those two had me. It wasn't the other way around. So they're stuck with me until I get ready to leave. Don't scowl like that. Probably you figured it out ages ago, how it is in my family, only you've got too much of Grandmother Reddick in you to come right out and believe that somebody couldn't care less about somebody else 'in the bloodline.' Isn't that her expression? That's what she said when she gave you that cruddy gold locket with the diamond in it. She just *knew* Junie would understand how she felt such a treasure had to go down in the 'bloodline.' Isn't that how it went?"

Taylor gave up hope of discussing her problems with Sandy. Maybe, though she'd never thought of it, she did have something of Grandmother's "family solidarity" notions. Not to the extent of caring about "bloodlines" or that awful gold locket. But something held her back from producing Tony and Junie like a bone to be nibbled at.

"I suppose we ought to start back," she said.

Drum, at that moment, rose to his feet, fur bristling along his back, lips curling. He gave a low steady growl, fixing his eyes on a pine tree at the edge of the woods. Looking up, Taylor caught her breath. There he was, the barred owl, sitting only a few feet above them, glaring downward. Far from being frightened by Drum, he appeared to be considering an attack. Taylor looked at him ecstatically, hardly daring to believe her luck.

"Hush," she whispered to Drum. "Don't scare him."

Drum barked. The owl let out a shriek of defiance and then on wide and soundless wings fled into the woods, still screaming.

"Oh wow," said Sandy. "He sounds like a gorilla."

"Isn't he beautiful? Just—simply beautiful?"

"Yeah, I guess he is at that. You should thank Drum, you know. If it hadn't been for him we would never have seen him."

Taylor, who'd been thinking that dumb Drum had driven the owl away, realized that Sandy was right. She reached down and patted the dog's head and the three of them started for the canoe and home.

~~nine

Riding on the mainland with Tony one day last spring, Taylor had spied a pair of sandhill cranes in a field.

"Tony, stop!" she'd cried out. "Right away!"

Having driven three children in automobiles for a number of years, he braked hastily, pulled to the verge of the road. "What's the matter, honey?" he asked, added, "You'd better get out—"

But Taylor was already out of the car, carrying her binoculars, walking slowly back along the verge to a good vantage point for observing the cranes. Not looking around, she beckoned with her arm for her father to follow.

"Look," she said softly, when he joined her. "Out there."

136

The cranes were performing their prenuptial dance. A strutting, shivering, crouching, leaping dance. They advanced, retreated, circled, came together with a loud clicking of bills, withdrew curvetting. All this was accompanied by the full-toned musical rattle of their call.

Taylor, giddy with delight, clutched her father's arm. "Tony! Do you believe it? Look at what we're looking at!"

Her father, as captivated as she, waited with her, watching, for a quarter of an hour or more. The birds were close enough to the road so that their joyful gavotte could be followed in all its intricacies, and Taylor did not use the glasses. The red bald bumpy head of the sandhill crane, observed closely, was no thing of beauty. What they were doing was beautiful beyond words, and Taylor did not intend to spoil the effect by a close view of what, from this distance, appeared to be a jaunty scarlet cap.

All at once it was over. The cranes moved apart and began to stalk across the field, sedately indifferent to each other.

Tony and Taylor watched them a while longer, then walked back to the car. Against the fence that bordered the field where the cranes had danced were discarded beer cans, cigarette packets, candy wrappers, even a large plastic bag of refuse that had burst open. As they started off, a camper sped by and a hand came out of the window, tossing a couple of paper cups that bounced on the road and came to rest on the grassy verge. It was followed by a half-pint milk container.

"The slobs shall inherit the earth," said Tony in a flat voice. "Or if the meek do, it'll be after the slobs have trashed it past living in."

A long silence, and then Taylor said, "They'll do it again, you know."

"You bet your tush they'll do it again."

"I meant the cranes. It takes a lot of dancing to get them turned on enough to mate. But I don't know that we'll be lucky enough ever to see it again."

"Taylor, tell me something. Do you actually not see all that's shitty around us? Small-bore pigs like those"—he gestured at the camper ahead—"or hogs on the big scale—phosphate miners, oil and lumber companies, developers—all junking the planet. Don't you *care*?"

"I care," she mumbled.

"Then what are you going to do about it?"

"Nothing."

"Nothing."

"What are you doing? Besides taking paper and cans to be recycled?"

"Nothing," he said after a while. "You're right. There's nothing to do, so that's what we'll do."

"You know what I wonder?" she said.

"What do you wonder, my nice girl?"

"If they remember dancing. The cranes. I mean, Tony, they looked so—so joyous, didn't they? Do you suppose it just slips out of their minds, once it's over?"

"All I know about birds is how to bone a duck. Taylor, try not to get obsessive. I know there's nothing to do about an obsession, but try not to be blinded to everything else in the world." When she didn't reply, he gave a short laugh and said, "Maybe you're the smart one, at that. Having one beautiful thing that blinds you to everything else. Do cranes remember their dance? That's one thing you ornithologists aren't ever going to find out. I hope they don't. Remembered ectasy should be a human burden."

"Burden?" said Taylor.

But he didn't take her up on that, and they drove the rest of the way—she couldn't remember now where they'd been going—in silence.

She hadn't seen the cranes dance again, but she thought about them now as she listened to her parents screaming downstairs. The cold silence hadn't lasted long, but she found no relief, as she'd thought she might, in their return to open, loud hostility. They didn't try at all to keep their quarrels private, as once they'd done. She could have gone down and walked right by without either of them noticing, probably. But she lay on her bed and listened, twisting her fingers together, turning her head once in a while on the pillow, not trying to shut out the sound of their voices. Whether she listened or not, they'd go on, and go on. . . .

There'd been a time when her parents had been sort of like the cranes dancing, joyous together. She could remember that. She couldn't quite remember when it had begun to stop. Had it stopped altogether? Weren't there times when they seemed anyway content together, a bit happy? When was the last time? Before the screen, she thought. Did people stop—did they stop *loving* each other because of something like that?

And if they did, what then?

What happened to her and to Jem and B.J.?

Other parents fought with each other. Family rooms all over the country were battlefields by day. Bedrooms, she supposed, were battlefields by night. People went their whole lives that way, some of them. It didn't mean anything except that married people didn't stay the same, didn't go on feeling joyous even if they'd started that way. That did not mean they were going to—

A burning broth rose in her throat. She had to swallow two or three times to get it down. I couldn't stand it, she thought, clenching her hands at her sides. I could not bear it if Tony and Junie got a divorce.

Who do they think they are, anyway? Don't they think about us at all when they're yelling about money and dancing in New York City and whether Junie was or wasn't going to get a job? When they yelled about whose fault everything was, did they ever think about their children? Didn't they think about anything but themselves?

"No!" she said aloud, sitting up. And then, to herself, *no, no, no, no* . . .

Let them fight and say all the horrible things they could think up, let them *hate* each other. "But they cannot get a divorce," she muttered out loud. "I won't allow them to do that."

I know what's going on in the world that's horrible, she answered her father's question of last spring. And I care. *And I can't do anything about any of it!*

"I can't do anything!" she screamed. So loud was her voice that the voices downstairs were stilled. In another moment her parents were at her door.

"Taylor," said her mother, coming to the bed, attempting to take her in her arms. "Taylor darling, you screamed. What's wrong?"

"Go away! Go away, both of you, and leave me alone!"

"But, Taylor," her father began. "We want to help. Are you sick or something?"

"You bet your tush I'm sick or something! Oh, go

away, go *away*. I'm tired, I tell you. I just want to lie here and be tired and—and be by myself. Let me *alone*, will you?"

She rolled around, pushing her face into the pillow. When she came up for air, they were gone.

~~*ten*

It was high tide. With mask, snorkel, fins and minnow net, Jem was swimming among the rocks at the back of Wrasse Island. The big tank was empty once again and he was looking for something interesting to stock it with. In the bait well on the skiff he had a baby octopus that had sprung out of an old horse conch shell on the mud flats a while earlier. The poor little thing had already squirted, in fear, its puny supply of ink. Jem planned to put it in the smaller tank until it calmed down enough to be put in the big one without clouding it. Or maybe he'd just leave it there and give it a couple of companions.

Adjusting the snorkel, he leaned into the water and swam slowly, looking this way and that. Schools of

143

tiny fish went past him—thousands and thousands of them maybe a sixteenth of an inch long. He'd get a bucketful of these for feeding his fish family later on, but just now he'd spied a little bitty mangrove snapper lurking in a rock crevice. Carefully he put the mouth of the minnow net against the hole, at the same time reaching around the rock with his other hand to flip water toward the snapper. Startled, it swam right into the deep net. Jem quickly squeezed enough of it to secure his captive, then stood and waded back to the skiff. Into the bait well with him. The well was so large and the octopus so small that the water was scarcely affected at all. Jem eyed with satisfaction the yellow-and-red snapper, decorated with what Taylor called black eyeliner. Very nice.

He turned back and continued his search.

An hour later, when he headed home, he had a cow-fish, a stingray, a purple sea anemone and a triggerfish in addition to the octopus and the snapper. He also had a bucket of food fish, and a rock with a stand of leaflike algae springing from it.

Dan was on the dock, looking grouchy. "Why didn't you call me before you went out?" he demanded.

The answer was Because I didn't think of it, but Jem said, "I did, and the line was busy." That was a safe excuse. Mrs. Howard was on the horn to her friends half the day.

144

"Catch," he said, throwing the line up. Then he handed up the anchor.

"Get something good?" Dan asked.

"Wait'll you see." Jem passed up the bucket of food fish and began transferring his finds into another pail, using a glass measuring jar.

Dan peered into the pail he was holding. The tiny fish were schooling. Round and round. They schooled when Jem put them in the tanks, too. Gradually the other fish would eat them. People who had fancy aquariums that they bought downtown also bought the fish they put in them. They bought the water and the substratum and coral or rocks for the fish to hide in. They bought the food they fed to their fish. But Jem had built his own tanks, with Tony's help, and he'd never bought a thing. The best food for fish is fish, he said, and every few days would go and get a bucketful of these teeny things, too small even to identify, to feed his larger fish, which were, of course, babies too. Sometimes he fed them minced raw scamp or grouper or something like that, but his fish preferred to catch their own meals.

"Would you help me to make an aquarium, Jem?"

"Sure. You always said you'd rather just look at mine."

"I've decided I'd like to have one of my own. If you help."

"My pleasure. Here, lookit this, Dan. A stingray."

He'd scooped up the ray in the quart measuring jar and now held it out for inspection. "Great, huh? Now lookit here. He's got his mouth on the bottom of his head, see. What I'm going to do is, I'm going to train him to do my bidding."

"Ah—cut it out."

"No kidding. I'm going to train him to do loops in the water at my command."

"Come on, Jem."

"You don't believe me." Jem laughed. "Okay, I'll tell you the secret, but don't tell anybody else, because maybe one day I'll take my trained ray to school and have him put on a show."

Dan, who still didn't know if he was having his leg pulled, listened attentively while Jem explained that the ray's mouth being on the bottom, he had to come around in a loop to get food from the surface. "What I'll do, see, is hold a bit of food just on the top of the water and he'll see it and come up and turn over so's he can grab it, and when he's done it enough times, I'll be able to make him loop even if I don't have any food in my hand. Like this—" He described a circle with his hand. "When he sees me do that, he'll just naturally loop around to get the food, and every third loop or so I'll really feed him. Same way you train a dog. Except I'll have a trained stingray."

"How did you ever think of that?" Dan asked,

breathtaken, as he so often was, by Jem's giant ingenuity.

"A mullet fisherman told me," Jem admitted. "A guy I met out back of Wrasse when I was snorkeling. Maybe it won't work, but we can try."

They went into the house, Jem carrying the aquarium fish and Dan the food fish, water slopping along the dock and then across the living room as they went. In Jem's room there were watermarks all over the floor where pails had been set down. Jem's bed was a tumbled mass of sheets and pillows. Books that had fallen out of the shelves lay where they'd landed. The shade on the bedlamp was broken and there were no curtains at the window, nor ever had been. Junie didn't hold with curtains. She said they reminded her of shrouds. Neither of the boys, occupied with something important, paid attention to the room.

First, with care, Jem lowered the rock into the water, adjusting it slightly off center so it would look nice. Then he and Dan sat back and looked at it. In the bubbling flow from the aerator, the algae leaves stirred gently. Looking closer, Jem saw that a little patch of coral formation was attached to the rock, and some minuscule oysters. As they watched, a couple of feather worms appeared almost magically, poking out of the rock, opening their little tips, like fringy parasols.

147

"Hey wow," said Dan. "Lookit that, will you. Did you know those were there when you got it?"

Jem shook his head. "They must have been inside. They're sessile, you know."

"What's sessile?"

"Attached. They're attached to the rock forever. Well, until the Conqueror Worm gets them."

The Conqueror Worm was death. Jem, who really liked all his fish, was fatalistic about losing some to what he called the Conqueror Worm. It was, to Dan's mind, a grand, strange expression and the sort of thing Jem came up with that made a person admire him hugely.

One by one the fish were transferred from the pail to their new, temporary home. The cowfish, little horns erect, began to describe helicopterlike motions, swimming backward, forward, hovering, descending, rising. The boys watched him for quite a while before putting the stingray in. Jem said training could wait while the ray got used to his surroundings. The sea anemone went in, drifting to the bottom, tentacles waving. It was like a beautiful flower. Then the triggerfish, and at last the food fish that began immediately to school again, darting and wheeling in formation as if, for all their numbers, they had to share a single mind. The octopus and the mangrove snapper went into the small tank where a rock taken from the larger tank, and an empty horse conch shell, could afford them refuge when they wanted it. They got a smaller number of food fish, and Jem put a glass lid on the tank so that the octopus could not crawl out.

Once, when Grandmother had been on a visit, Jem had come into the living room where she was looking at television.

Jem: My octopus escaped.

Grandmother Reddick: Your octopus? Oh dear. How do you suppose he did that?

Jem: Guess he just crawled up the side of the tank and tipped out. Poor little guy. I've looked for him everywhere.

Grandmother Reddick: Can he climb stairs?

Jem: I don't think so. I mean, I don't see how he could, do you? You mean he might get into your bedroom?

Grandmother Reddick: Well, I—

Jem: If you do find him, give me a call right away, will you?

Grandmother Reddick: I can promise you that. What do you do if you can't find him?

Jem: Well, nothing. What can I do?

The Conqueror Worm got the octopus and they found him by the smell.

"It's funny," Jem said now, looking with pleasure at the red-and-yellow snapper swimming over the octopus, which had not yet released any ink so perhaps could be considered content with its new home. "It's funny how they don't seem to mind being caught and dumped in these tanks. They had the whole entire bay to navigate and now here they are in *tanks*, and you'd think they'd be fighting mad. If I got put in something the same size, for my size I mean, and didn't know I was going to be let out again soon, I'd be throwing myself against those glass walls till I knocked them down or myself out."

"You aren't a fish," Dan pointed out. He sounded serious, so Jem said, "Yeah, there's that," and didn't smile.

The floor around the tanks was drenched. The boys in their bare feet had tracked water around the rest of the room, and somehow Jem's sheet had moved over into a puddle so that one whole corner was sopping.

"Let's clean up here a bit," said Jem.

"I gotta split. My old man says we gotta be home for lunch every day. He takes roll call." He looked at his friend anxiously. "If it wasn't for that, I'd help for sure."

"It's okay. How long is he going to keep that up?"

Dan lifted his shoulders. "Who the hell knows?" As he was leaving, Jem called after him, "You talking to that doctor yet?"

"Nope," yelled Dan, and was gone.

Jem went into the bathroom, got some towels and mopped up, pulled the wet sheet off his bed and carried the bundle to the laundry room, where he dumped it in the hamper. He sniffed. The whole room smelled sour. He leaned over the hamper. Pukey. Somebody ought to do a washing.

He started back to look some more at his new fish and realized for the first time since getting home that the house was awfully quiet. His mother might be at one of her yoga sessions, but where were the rest of them? There'd been no one on the dock when he came in from Wrasse Island. He glanced out the window, saw that the boats were in place. Tony's car was gone, but not the station wagon.

He stood at the foot of the stairs, listening, finally mounted and went to the door of his parents' room. Junie was at the closet with her back to him. On the bed was piled a whole bunch of clothes, and there were two suitcases open, one on the bed, one on the luggage stand. The one on the bed was nearly full of stuff.

Jem stood, taking this in, then said, "What are you doing?"

His mother jumped, whirled, hand over her heart.

151

"Jem! Oh my word, you *startled* me." She sat down, half smiling. "The startle of my life. My heart's thumping."

"What are you doing?"

"Well, love—as you see. I'm packing."

"For what?"

She turned aside, took a cigarette, lit it and blew smoke out. Her hands were unsteady. And Tony's car gone. Another fight, then. Jem wondered, really wondered, if they didn't ever get tired of it. It must be a hassle, having to yodel down the warpath over and over, and then make up over and over, and then find a reason to start up again. Or, he admitted, they didn't have to find reasons. Reasons fell in their laps like coconuts dropping on the ground. But always, now, as soon as one battle had rumbled away in the distance like a storm moving out to sea, a new one moved up. It was like waiting for hurricanes, and he did not see how, at their age, they had the stamina for it.

"What are you packing for?" he repeated.

"Don't *push* me, Jem."

"I'm not pushing. I'm asking."

"Well, give me a chance to answer."

He sat on the edge of a rocker, not letting it rock, and waited.

Junie licked her lips with a little flick of her tongue,

gave him that half smile again, took a long drag on her cigarette, stubbed it out, looked at him with an air of decision. "I'm taking a trip."

"Where?"

"New York."

"New York City?"

"Oh lordy, you sound just like your father." He continued to stare at her. "Will you stop looking at me that way, Jem? You wanted to know what I'm doing and I told you. Now what?"

"I want to know why you're going."

"Look, Jem. You are my son, not my husband or my keeper. I love you devotedly, but I am not required to explain my every move to you."

"Does Tony know you're going to New York City?"

"Yes. No. I don't know. He stormed out of here without giving me a chance to discuss anything with him."

"So he doesn't know."

"Just who do you think you are, Jem, quizzing me like counsel for the prosecution? Other women take trips here and there without having to file with the commissars. When did I last go anywhere? Give me an answer to that, if you can. When have I, in your recollection, gone farther from home than a merry jaunt to Tallahassee?"

"You mean you're just going to take those suitcases and get in your car and go to New York City before Tony even gets back?"

Junie looked at him levelly. "As it happens, that is precisely what I mean. I am going to take a little trip, without or with the sanction of my husband."

"Can't you wait and talk it over with him?"

"I *tried* to talk it over with him. He went out of here like a smoke bomb—a *saffron*-colored smoke bomb. Jem—don't you think *I* have any rights? Don't you think a woman is entitled to do something on her own, *just once in a while*?"

"It sounds to me like running away. When are you coming back?"

"Soon."

"When?"

"I don't know! I said soon. That's enough. Will you stop biting your fingernails?"

Jem snatched his thumb from his mouth. He was feeling horrible. Sick. If he said so, she'd think he was making it up to keep her here. He couldn't believe, not really believe, that his mother was going to do this. What *was* so awful about taking a trip? She was right. Other people—other women—took trips. They went away, without their husbands, to visit relatives and things. He couldn't make himself feel that this trip was like those trips.

"You gonna visit somebody?"

"Daddy's brother, Jim. You remember him."

"No."

"Oh, Jem. He was here—well, it must've been quite a while ago at that. I guess," she said slowly, "not since Daddy's funeral." She looked around pensively, as if surprised to find herself where she was. "Quite a while ago," she said again, and drew a deep breath. "Uncle Jim has law offices in New York. *City*. On Wall Street. And a nice house in Connecticut. He's been asking me for years to visit. I mean, he's been asking us. He wants all of us to come and see him."

"First I've heard of it."

"You're beginning to sound like a damn policeman."

He sounded like counsel for the prosecution, like his father, like a policeman. Like a commissar. He did not know what a commissar was, and didn't care.

"Then why aren't we going with you?" he asked.

For a moment he thought she was going to scream, but then she said quietly enough, "Because, Jem, I want to do something by myself for a change. That's something you should be able to understand. Who likes to take the skiff out and go skin diving alone? Who takes the canoe out on the bay, by himself, at sunset, and *wants to be* by himself?"

"That's different. I'm always coming back."

"Jem!"

"I can't help it. It's the feeling I get about"—he

waved his hand at the closet, the suitcases—"about all this. It doesn't *feel* like somebody coming back."

One of Junie's daddy's sayings, according to her, was that a boat running before the wind had an easier time of it than a boat tacking into the wind. It hardly came out to a "saying." It was just common sense, and it meant it's easier to run away than to come back. He really was feeling sick.

"I'm going downstairs," he said. He went to his room and lay face down on the rumpled bed. He heard his mother come down with a suitcase, heard her go outside, heard the slam of the station wagon door. She came back for the other case. Then there was silence for a while. No car starting. No nothing. All he could hear was the fan over the dining room table. It was beginning to squeak and ought to be oiled.

He sensed when she came to his door and stood waiting for him to turn and look at her, but he didn't move. In a moment she walked over, leaned down and kissed the back of his head. "I've left a note for Tony on the coffee table. Jem? Jem, please look at me." They waited, each unmoving. Then, "Well. Well . . . anyway, tell your father where my note is. I love you." She stopped again at the door. "I always seem to be leaving my children prone on beds. Or is it supine? Do you know the difference, Jem? Between prone and supine?"

156

He didn't move. In a few minutes he heard the station wagon go slowly out of the driveway. So slowly that he thought maybe she was going to stop and turn around and come back. But she didn't.

⌁eleven

When Taylor came in an hour later with B.J., Jem
was doing a washing.

"For Pete's sake," she said. "What's got into you?"

"Where've you two been?"

"At the beach. They started another home dis-
cussion period, so I took B.J. kite-flying. He shouldn't
have to hear that—listen to that—all the time."

"He won't have to anymore."

"What's that supposed to mean?"

The spin cycle stopped. Jem shoved the clothes into
the dryer, turned it on, turned to face his sister.

"What's wrong?" she said. "Jem, *what is it*? B.J.,
go find Drum, will you?"

"He's right here," said B.J., pointing.

"Then take him out on the dock and give him a hosing. Be sure to put the spray nozzle on."

B.J. hesitated. But he did love to hose down Drum, so he nodded and went off, followed by his dog.

Taylor looked at her brother and waited.

"She's gone." His voice sounded squeaky. "She left a note for Tony. I read it."

"What—what's it say?" she whispered.

"That she's gone to visit her Uncle Jim."

"Who's that?"

"Her daddy's brother. He came for the funeral."

"Where is he? In Tampa?"

"In New York City."

"What are you *talking* about? She can't have just taken off for New York *City* without telling anybody."

"She told in the note. She says she has to get away and have some space and think things over and be by herself and she loves us."

Taylor ran into the living room, snatched the note up, read it once quickly and once again, slowly. It said what Jem said it said. She put it carefully back in the clutter on the coffee table, and sat on the sofa. Her heart was racing around, as if it had got loose in her chest. She could feel pulses going all over her body, even at the back of her neck, and she found it hard to get a deep breath. She had her mouth open, trying to drag in air, when Jem came in and sat on a chair across from her. He looked at her carefully, but didn't say anything, and so they sat in silence until B.J., carrying a wet and squirming Tut, came into the house from the dock.

"He got hosed, too. I don't think he likes it."

"Maybe you better get a towel and dry him," Taylor said, but Tut managed to wriggle loose and run under the sofa.

B.J. looked at his brother and sister. "I hosed Drum down good," he said. "I guess he likes it better than anything." After a little while, he said, "I'm hungry."

As he spoke they heard the sound of a car coming down the driveway. The flicker of hope died as it rose. You could always tell Tony's VW from their mother's station wagon.

"Ah, gee," said Jem. "Now what happens?"

"Taylor, I said I'm hungry."

"Go get yourself a banana."

"I don't want a banana."

Taylor jumped up, ran for the kitchen, leaving Jem in the living room to face Tony, returned almost immediately. "I guess we better be together," she said, as her father pulled up beside the house and stopped.

Tony, usually quick and light-footed, seemed to take a long time getting out of his car, and when he came in, moved heavily.

"Hi, kids," he said. "Where's your mother?"

B.J. came out of the kitchen eating a banana and scowling. "I don't want a banana," he told Taylor crossly. "I want milk toast."

"You'll have to wait."

"But I don't want to—"

"Shut up, B.J."

Astonished at his sister's tone, B.J. stopped talking. He spied his father and launched himself forward. "Tony, I want milk toast and she won't give it to me!"

"Taylor doesn't have to do everything you say, B.J. I'll make you some. It's way past lunchtime anyway, isn't it? How about chocolate milk toast all around?" He looked at Taylor and Jem. "What's up? Hey now, look—something's wrong here and I want to know what it is. What are you two up to?"

"*We* aren't up to anything," Taylor said. "There's a note there for you. On the table."

Looking again from one to the other of his elder children, Tony moved slowly to the coffee table, looked down, stood reading the note without picking it up. He read, or stared at it, for a long time, then sat, elbows on his knees, hands across his mouth, eyes closed.

"How could she?" he said at last. "How could she do this to us?"

"Tony! You said chocolate milk toast all around!"

"Yeah. Sure thing, B.J." He stared across the room.

"She needs space. She needs time to think things over. Come on, B.J., I'll fix you that milk toast. You two want some?"

Taylor and Jem shook their heads.

"He's angry," Jem said, when their father and brother had gone into the kitchen. "Not sad. *Angry.*" His face darkened.

"You don't know that. You can't tell how someone else is feeling. Anyway—why shouldn't he be angry? Aren't you?" When Jem didn't reply, she said, "See that thing on the wall there?"

"What thing?"

"That new picture."

Jem looked at the crowded wall of pictures. Junie replaced one thing with another from time to time, often having to draw people's attention to her changes. It took a moment for Jem to find the new one. A print, or an etching or something, of two fish skeletons. He got up and stood in front of it for a closer study. One fish's head was rammed into the other's mouth. Could be groupers or any big-mouthed fish, Jem thought. They did that sometimes, tried to eat each other up.

"It's an intaglio," Taylor said. "She got it at a barn sale."

It seemed to Jem just the sort of thing Junie would pick up. She loved the skeletons of fish. "So delicate," she'd said to him once. "So marvelously formed.

Really, Jem, the perfect arrangement of bones, a fish's."

"Junie met the artist," Taylor said. "A girl. She actually found the skeleton, I mean the two skeletons, on the beach. One fish choked to death and the other one smothered. That's what started the fight. I mean, *their* fight." When Jem didn't speak, she added, "Junie was putting it up in place of that picture of a church in Italy and Tony came in and—" She stopped. She didn't want to tell. Anyway, Jem could fill in the blanks with no trouble.

Tony: Now what?

Junie: What do you mean, now what?"

Tony: Now, what have we here? That's what I mean.

Junie: We have here a very inexpensive but marvelous intaglio of fish bones. See, these two fish had at each other, each trying to gobble the other down, and look what they came to. Once they clashed, neither had a chance. Not a chance. The young woman who did this—I think she's talented, don't you?—quite unimaginatively called it Death by Water.

Tony: And you call it?

163

Junie: Oh, there's only one possible title for this. Marriage.

That started the worst fight between them that Taylor had heard so far. Vicious. She listened long enough to know it was going to last and grow worse, and then, putting B.J. and a kite on the back of her bike, had gone over to the beach for a couple of hours. Even when they'd come back, she'd approached the house cautiously and, then, finding both the station wagon and the VW gone, had come into the house breathing more easily. She had not expected that this time they'd make up with kisses very fast. It had, recently, taken them longer and longer to get to that part after a quarrel. She'd just been relieved that neither of them was home.

And now . . . and now what?

Tony came back and sat where he had before, leaning forward, elbows on his knees again. This time he moved the skin of his forehead round and round with the tips of his fingers. That way he could talk without looking at them.

"I have to go to work. There's . . . there's a dinner tonight—" He stopped, resumed. "A dinner for the— the governor of the state. He's bringing a party of twelve, and I'm . . . I am—" He sat up, looked at the fan over the dining room table. "I am cooking this dinner. By request." He looked at them. "Junie knew about it." He fingered his mustache, one side, then the other. "Forgot, I suppose." He stood up. "We'll have to try to figure out something tomorrow. If she—Well, we'll see. Tomorrow. I'm going up and change."

When he came down Jem and Taylor were sitting where he'd left them. B.J. was on the floor, counting his marbles, but looking up suspiciously now and then. B.J. knew how to put first things first. That being, of course, his own interests. But he was sensitive to atmosphere and did not care for the one he was in.

"Look, kids," Tony said. "Things will work out. Okay?"

"Sure, Tony," Taylor said.

Tony glanced at Jem, hesitated. The room was getting dark. "There's going to be a storm. Can you see to the boats? I don't have time. I'm late already."

Taylor walked out to the car with him. As he turned on the ignition and twisted his head in order to see to back up, Taylor bent over and kissed him. "I love you, Tony."

Her father closed his eyes, opened them, nodded without speaking. She stepped away to allow him room to back, then shouted, "Good luck with the governor's dinner!" He waved, and was gone.

When Jem had come in with his new fish the sky had been bluely bright, with big clouds white and still as soap sculpture. That had been only a couple of hours ago? A little longer, maybe? Seemed like another world, another part of time and the world, when he and Dan had crossed the living room with the pails sloshing and all he'd had to worry about was slopped water and whether his fish would take to their new surroundings. Now, over the bay, great cloud banks stood, sinister grey-black clouds, edged silvery white, the color of that mother-of-pearl on Junie's table. He could hear the growling rumble of the Gulf of Mexico. The bay waters slapped under their dock. The wind groaned in branches high above them, setting the palm fronds streaming, the bamboos swaying. The bamboos in the wind creaked and sighed with a hollow sound, and faraway thunder lurched out of the sky. It had a battlefield sound. Now a skywide web of lightning flashed, and the first tremendous drops came splashing down.

He and Taylor dragged *Merrywing* well back, and then the canoe, turning them over on the sand. Jem ran down the dock to check the lines of *Loon*, came back and leaped into the skiff to make sure those lines too were secure.

He came into the house, peeling off his shirt.

"You're soaked," Taylor said. She was sitting on the floor beside B.J.'s bed. "Why don't you take a warm shower?"

"He under there?"

"They both are. And Tut's still under the sofa. It's

an instinct, I guess. To hide under something when danger threatens."

"Maybe you and I should get under mine," he said, attempting a smile.

Taylor, with an effort, smiled back. "I hope they're all right," she said. "Driving in this rain."

Jem went into the bathroom and closed the door without answering. Presently she heard the rush of shower water through the sound of rain lashing against the windows and the far-off pounding in the Gulf of waves against reefs.

Then there was the sound that always came almost as soon as a storm began. Sirens. Ambulance or fire engine, shrieking down the island. To Taylor they seemed like bloody streamers, tatters flying through the air like fish entrails in a gull's fierce beak. She hated sirens. And driving in the rain like this was horrible. She hoped that Tony, late or not, would pull over to the side of the road, because she knew, as if she were in the car with him, that his windshield would have an impenetrable waterfall streaming down it. Surely, late or not, he'd pull over. He has to think of us, she told herself. He *knows* he has to think of us, and being late, even for a governor, doesn't matter. She tried to force this thought upon him, wherever he was, driving down the island in the storm. Where was that ambulance, or siren, going?

She wouldn't wonder, wouldn't think.

"You okay, B.J.?" she said. Drum's tail thudded the only response from under the bed.

Junie, by now, could be past the storm breaking over their heads here. She could be heading north in a day still bright with sunshine, on her way to the time and space she said she needed.

~~twelve

When the storm was over the sun came out, sudden and brilliant. Puddles sank into the sandy earth, the dock steamed, a layer of mist curled over the bay, evaporating slowly. Some branches had gone down, and the shell driveway was littered with leaves and pine needles. B.J. and Drum came out from under the bed and went about their pursuits as if foreign to fear.

Taylor thought of phoning Sandy and then did not. She'd have to explain and she didn't know what to explain. Didn't know how.

"Why?" Jem asked when she said this to him. "Explain why? I mean, what? Our mother's gone on a trip. Plenty of mothers go on trips. She'll be back."

"Jem, stop biting your nails. It's so awful."

"I know." But he didn't stop. "How long do you suppose she'll stay away?"

"Maybe forever," Taylor said angrily, expecting, rather hoping, that Jem would get angry with her. She felt a twisting inner anguish that shouting or crying might relieve. If they could yell at each other, or throw something, break something, or cry . . . if they could *cry*.

But Jem just held his arms tight across his chest and stared at her.

"Do you—would you like some lemonade?" she asked.

"Yeah. That'd be fine."

They went into the kitchen. Taylor sat on the high stool while Jem got lemons from the icebox, got the squeezer out, got a knife.

He put the knife down and turned, shaking his head. "It's too much trouble." He walked out on the dock, threw himself on a chair, kicked his heels a moment, then grew entirely still. His mouth was thin and white and tight, his eyes blank.

Taylor made the lemonade and brought him a glass, then sat on the swing, sipping. After a while she said, "Jem—for as long as—well, as long as she's gone— we're going to have to—to exist, you know. We have to move about and do things." When he didn't respond, she went on. "Cook, you know. Even people who aren't especially hungry have to eat something. And there's B.J. He needs to be fed. We have to take care of him, you know. We can't just stop *existing*."

"Go ahead and exist. Nobody's stopping you."

"Don't be childish."

"I'll be childish if I want to be and you can't stop me."

"And you can't do this to me. Or to Tony."

"Screw Tony."

"Stop it this minute! Don't you talk that way, hear?"

"*He's* the reason she's gone."

"He is not! She's gone because of something in *her*."

"She's gone because of what he did. Stopping her from spending a little money—"

"A little money? Do you know what that screen *cost*?"

"I don't want to hear from you what anything cost. You got that? And everything's his fault. Every damn thing is *his* fault. Never letting her have any fun, yelling at her all the time, never taking her out anywhere—"

"She did every bit as much yelling as he did, you stupid creep! And she didn't spend a little bit of money, she used up practically everything in his savings account. I bet that's what she's gone to New York on—"

"Don't you say that! You're making it up!"

"I am not making it up. I *heard*. He went to the
bank and there was nothing, just about *nothing* left.
Tony said there was a couple of thousand dollars last
time he looked and then he went to get some and there
wasn't even a hundred. That is *not* a little bit of
money!"

"You're against her!" Jem shouted. "You're against
your own mother, you grungy fink!"

Taylor threw her glass against the wall. It smashed,
throwing lemonade and splinters over Jem.

"Oh, Jem," she cried out. "Oh, honey—I'm sorry.
I'm *sorry*. Are you cut? Are you all right? I didn't
mean to do it—"

Jem delicately brushed bits of glass from his arm.
"It's okay. I shouldn't have said that. Maybe it's in-
heritable, screaming and throwing things."

Taylor went for wet paper towels and a brush and
dustpan. As she cleaned up, she said, "We can't do this,
you know. We'll scare B.J."

"He hasn't even noticed she's gone."

"Be reasonable, Jem. It's only been a few hours.
She's often gone far longer than this. Why should he
notice yet? But Jem, don't you see—with Tony gone
or asleep a good part of the day, we have—we have to
take care of ourselves. And him."

"Like those kids in *Lord of the Flies*."

"Don't *say* that," she snapped. "We are not in the
least like those—those horrible creepy kids."

"Don't jump on me. I didn't really read it. I just started it, and got bored. I mean, what was it all about? How did they make out on that island?"

"They were—horrible," she said again.

"Even Ralph? He seemed kind of nice. In the beginning, anyway."

"He and Piggy tried—tried to keep—standards," she said, Grandmother's word again. "They didn't have a chance."

"Was there really a beast on the island?"

"No. Yes. They were the beast, themselves. All except Ralph and Piggy."

"Who was the Lord of the Flies?"

"A pig's head stuck on a stick, with flies eating it. That was the Lord of the Flies."

"Did that mean anything? I mean, I expect it all meant something. Junie says it's a classic. But I don't know—I like Robinson Crusoe. What was the Lord of the Flies supposed to be?"

Taylor shook her head. "Evil, I guess. Maybe the devil. I couldn't make out. I hated that book."

"I'm glad I don't have to finish books I hate just because I started reading them. Why don't you stick to bird books?"

"I mostly do."

She'd picked up *Lord of the Flies* at Sandy's and had begun reading because at the moment she'd had nothing else to do. It had closed on her like the pincers of a giant crab and until she'd finished, she'd been unable to realize the world around her. She'd wanted to skip and had not been able to. She'd read every horrible, cruel, stomach-grinding line, and when she was done hadn't been able to get it out of her mind for days. Even now, when she thought of it, she shivered. Because the book was real. It wasn't a fantasy. It was what happened. It was people trashing the earth, it was men going into the Everglades with guns and shooting things in that "protected" wilderness. It was kids riding minibikes over terns' eggs, and kids shooting heroin, fornicating at age twelve, committing suicide. It was grown-ups marrying and walking out on their marriages. It was wars. People killing other people all over the world. Wars, for as long as people had existed.

"Do you ever think about war, Jem?"

"No."

A ten-year-old American kid didn't need to think about war. There were boys Jem's age all over the world who had never known anything else. The most he'd ever had to worry about was whether his sargassum fish would eat his groupers. Until today. Now, no matter how many times he said she'd gone on a little trip, underneath he was worried, the same way she was, wondering if Junie had gone on a trip or had just plain split and wasn't ever coming home again.

In the morning a telegram came. "Not to worry. Will be in touch. Love you all. Junie."

Tony read it, handed it to Taylor, who read and handed it to Jem. He read it carefully before dropping it on the table next to her note. No one made a comment.

After that they didn't hear for a week. It seemed strange to Taylor that in just a week everything could come so apart.

~~thirteen

A toy piano came crashing down the hall, skidding from wall to wall, coming to rest in a tinkle of scattered keys. The little bench came after it, thudding, dropped clinking among the ruins.

"Do you hear me?" B.J. shouted. "I'm breaking things!"

Taylor and Jem looked at each other. "Let's ignore him," she said. "He'll get tired after a while."

"After how much else gets broken?"

There was a tremendous crash and they shot from their chairs and hurtled down the hall to Jem's room, where their small brother, red-faced and wet with sweat, stood over the lamp he'd dashed to the floor.

"Now I'm gonna throw your tank over!" he yelled

at Jem, and turned to lay hands on the smaller of the two tanks.

Jem sprang at him. Grabbing the thin arms, he shook B.J. like a mop. "You touch those tanks and you'll—I'll—don't you dare lay a paw on my tanks, you understand?"

B.J.'s head was wobbling as Taylor rushed at Jem and grabbed a hunk of his hair. "Let go of him, Jem! Stop that! You'll hurt him!"

"Hurt him? I'm gonna kill him!"

"Jem, stop this minute! He's a little boy, he's a *baby*. You don't know your own strength! Let him *go*, I tell you!"

Jem released his hold and B.J. fell to the floor. As Taylor pulled him away from the broken lamp pieces and tried to hold him in her arms, he hit her across the face. For his age, he had punch.

Taylor took a deep breath. A baby, he was only a baby. "B.J., listen to me—"

"You smelly sea cucumber! I'm gonna kill you both!"

"You see," Taylor snarled over her shoulder. "You see what comes of talking that way? Just because he admires you and tries to imitate you—"

"I don't admire him! I don't imitate him! The fool jackass, I'm gonna push him in the bay!"

"What are we going to do?" Taylor moaned.

"Get away get away get away," B.J. howled. "I

don't want you!" He narrowed his eyes at Jem. "And I don't want you, too!"

Taylor put a tentative hand toward him. He hit it away. "Get out! I don't want you!"

"Do you think we should call Tony?" Jem asked.

"At the restaurant? What could he do from there? We'd just get him upset. B.J., *please*—stop doing this to us. Please, B.J. Be a big boy."

B.J. sat, legs stretched out, beating his heels on the floor, pushing his balled fists into his eyes. "I want Junie," he sobbed, and leaned over so that his head touched the boards between his legs. "I want my mother. . . ."

It had taken him two days and nights to realize that Junie had gone, had left him without saying good-bye. Since then, he'd been inconsolable and uncontrollable, unless Tony was around. Until his father left for work he was sulky but subdued. By the time Tony got back around midnight B.J. had, so far, fought and screamed and whined his way into prostrated whimpering sleep. And, so far, Taylor and Jem had said nothing to their father of what the afternoons and evenings had become.

In any case, Tony, absorbed, absentminded, withdrawn, did not seem to be taking much notice of his children.

Not fair, Taylor said to herself. Not *fair*. He acts as if Jem and I were some grown-up couple he'd hired to take care of his house and child. He acts as if Jem and I were his *wife*, with no choice except to put up with this rotten kid.

Junie: Marriage is a compromise, Taylor. Always remember that. Two people get married, and the woman starts compromising.

Taylor: But Junie. It can't always be that way.

Junie: There may be exceptions, but I have not, personally and with my own eyes, seen one. If the man likes to play bridge, the woman learns to play bridge. If she likes to play bridge and he doesn't, she stops playing. If he golfs and she ever wants to see him, she learns to play golf. If she golfs and he thinks it's a stupid waste of time, she quits playing. And so it goes—into every nook and cranny of their lives together, the details of which I'll spare you. Just thought I'd give you this bit of housewife's hindsight insight. It just might give you some foresight.

When B.J. had shuddered into silence, Jem said, "I think I'll take *Merrywing* out for a sail. There's a

179

good offshore breeze, wouldn't you say, B.J.?"

B.J. looked up. His nose was running. Taylor resisted the impulse to hand him a tissue as he put his tongue out to tidy up. He looked from his brother to his sister, wiped his nose with the back of his hand, wiped his hand on his thigh. "Is Drum going?"

"Doesn't he always?"

"Not always. Once you wouldn't let him. You told him, 'Stay, Drum!' You upset him."

"Well, I won't upset him today." Jem sighed. "I want him to come. How about it, Taylor. You coming?"

"No, that's all right. You two go along. I mean, if you *want* to, B.J."

The thought of being without him for a couple of hours was like cool water on her head in the midst of a sunstruck day. It was like a glass of ginger ale with little chips of ice in it after hours of dry thirst. Simply put, it sounded like heaven. And if he chose not to go, it would be hell. It was that elementary.

"Okay," said B.J., getting to his feet.

Jem looked at the mess on the floor. "I hate to leave you with all this to clear up."

"Don't give it a thought. It's my pleasure. I'll have it all tidied up and I'll have supper ready and—"

"Don't get hysterical," Jem said in a dry tone. "You aren't being sprung. Just getting an hour or so off."

180

"For good behavior?"

He grinned. "C'mon, B.J. See you, Taylor."

"Jem?"

He turned at the end of the hall.

"Thank you."

"It's okay. You can do something for me some day."

They were gone.

Taylor stepped over the broken lamp, walked past the broken piano and the little piano stool, went upstairs, passing her parents' room without a glance, climbed the short flight of stairs to her room at the top. She lay down on her bed and fell asleep.

The telephone jangling downstairs wakened her and she stumbled to the second floor, into her parents' room, and picked it up.

"Taylor?"

"Hi, Sandy."

"You sound funny."

"I was asleep."

"Oh. Sorry."

"No, no, no. I'm glad you woke me up. I want to be conscious of being alone."

"Well, in that case—"

"I didn't mean you. These days, being alone means being without B.J., to me."

"Say, what's going on over there? I've phoned a zillion times and yesterday I came by, and the place is like a plague had struck it. I haven't heard from you in days. Is somebody sick or something?"

Taylor leaned over and blew dust off the bedside table. She straightened a few books. What she owed was loyalty to her family. What she needed was Sandy to talk to. "Could you come over now? Tony made apricot bars."

"You don't have to bribe me," Sandy said crisply. "The kind with pistachio nuts?"

"Yes," said Taylor.

She put the broken piano and stool back in B.J.'s corner, because he'd raise Cain if she threw them out. She swept up the lamp base, put the shade in the hall closet, got another lamp from the living room for Jem's table. No matter what time they got to bed, she and Jem always had to read before they went to sleep. Junie was like that, too.

She went out to wait for Sandy, wandering idly along the point where mangroves stood tall as trees. A black-whiskered vireo was singing in there, a drawn-out call, not varied, but sweet. Not as sweet as the song of the meadowlark. Oh, the song of the meadow-lark! How brilliant he was, with his yellow breast, black-necklaced. How his melody stayed in her thoughts, like chimes, after she'd heard him. The black-whiskered vireo, as if sensing her unfair comparison, flickered out of the mangroves and swayed on a twig almost before her eyes. A friendly fellow, the vireo. Then she heard another call, above her head. A quick, descending chatter. Glancing up, she saw a summer tanager in the silk oak tree. A life bird! A bird for her life list, and she'd spotted him as easily as a dove on a telephone wire. Because she'd happened to walk out here, just at this moment. He was beautiful, a sleek, small, dusty-rose bird. He dipped his head down, regarding her with eyes black as black coral beads, and was gone. But the vireo went on singing.

Taylor patted the trunk of the silk oak, smiling a bit. It was certainly a bird-luring tree, even now. In springtime, when its soft, frondy, yellow blossoms hung limp and fragrant, it seemed to draw to its bower and make drunk with joy every sort of warbler there was. They drank from its blossoms, and sang their little tails off because the silk oak was in bloom again.

When Sandy biked in and skidded to a stop, Taylor said, "I just saw a summer tanager."

"Good time for him to be around."

"But I never saw one before."

"Oh, hey. Another one for the list. That's neat." Sandy always managed to get up enthusiasm for other people's enthusiasms. She said it wasn't because she was always—actually hardly ever—interested in what they were interested in. Birds, or motorcycles, or tennis, or the novels of Kerouac—whatever. But she was interested in how interested people *were* in different things. "Imagine," she'd say, "actually caring how the United States makes out in the Olympic games. I mean, it's freaky. But nice, you know. And all those kids at school minding who wins a basketball game." She wasn't being superior. She really thought it was cute and appealing that every weekend crowds of kids and even grown-ups yelled themselves hoarse for the local team playing whatever it happened, for the season, to be playing. So now she greeted Taylor's news of the summer tanager with pleasure.

"How many does that make?" she asked, when they were on the porch with iced tea. "Oh, boy—Tony's apricot bars."

"A hundred and forty-seven, I guess," Taylor said indifferently. The summer tanager, the life list—who cared?

"Something's wrong, huh?" said Sandy.

But she couldn't talk about it. She'd wanted to, she needed to, she couldn't. "How's Amanda?" she asked with effort.

"Oh, wow. Well, either Dr. Borden got to them, or Amanda made some more threats or something not in my hearing, but the end *result* is, she's allowed to have this boyfriend, this Alexander. Well, sixteen. She ought to have one. It's good experience. But Alex-*ander*—"

"What's he like?"

"Hoo, you'd never believe. She brings him home, because my father says young ladies do not meet their acquaintances at McDonald's and hang around the parking lot. I like that young ladies, don't you? Actually, he's given in a lot, and even Amanda knows when to stop pushing. So the guy's practically boarding with us, and Amanda bats her eyes and languishes at him like Elizabeth Barrett Browning, and he almost doesn't look at her but that's, I think, because he knows the old man's eye is upon him. Every second. I think my mother is keeping vodka in her eau de cologne bottle. She loathes him."

"Is he so awful?"

"So unchic you can hardly believe. Like a living artifact of the sixties. He has a ponytail. When did you last see a ponytail on a guy? Except the kind that gets stoned all the time. He talks about silicone people and the Establishment. Quaint, you know? But apparently the best Amanda can do for a first try. They eat carob pods together. I think. Anyway, nothing that'll give them a buzz, like mushrooms. He isn't into that sort of thing."

"How do you know?"

"It shows, if it's bad enough. Anyway, my father had him looked into."

"He *did*?"

"Well, sure. Amanda's his little princess in the tower. You don't think he's going to let her entertain some redneck from Plant City."

Taylor could hear Mr. Howard saying it. "What did he find when he looked into him?"

"My dear," Sandy said, imitating her father addressing her mother. "*My* dear, we have *nothing* to worry about. The boy's father is on the Boards of four companies, and the boy himself is slated for Princeton. He's just going through a phase." Sandy shifted on the swing, altered her voice and became her mother. "But he's such an em*barrassment*—every time I look at him I want to curl up and *die*. I believe I'll just go up and pat a little eau de cologne on my forehead and lie down."

"You honestly think your mother is drinking?"

"Sure, I honestly think it. I mean, I know she is, right up front. I'm not entirely sure about the eau de cologne bottle, but it seems funny that anyone could get that smashed every day on two drinks at lunch and two before dinner."

"You don't mind?"

"Taylor, over and over I tell you—what they do does not concern me."

"Would you like to be in a world without grown-ups?" Taylor asked, thinking again of *Lord of the Flies*.

186

"No. They sort of keep things in order. Cops, teachers, even parents to some extent. I would *not* want to be without teachers, because I don't think I could learn everything on my own."

"You surprise me."

"Sarcasm, Taylor, has never withered me."

"I don't think anything could wither you," Taylor muttered.

"You sound as if you want something to."

"How would you like it if your mother ran away?" Taylor flung out at her.

"I wouldn't mind."

Taylor burst into tears.

Sandy waited awhile, then put a tentative hand on her friend's shoulder. "Oh, hey," she said softly. "Is that what happened?"

"Junie doesn't live here anymore," Taylor sobbed. "She's gone. She just walked out on us and is—gone."

"Where to?"

Taylor, like B.J., wiped her nose with the back of her hand.

"Here," said Sandy, handing over her paper napkin. "Use this."

"Thanks."

"Gone where?"

"New York City. Her Uncle Jim. That's her daddy's brother. And don't tell me you wouldn't mind if it was your mother."

"Honestly, Taylor, I wouldn't. Why should I? I mean, your mother's nicer than mine, but just the same—what's the big deal? She's told you in fifty thousand ways that she didn't think she ought to be a mother *or* married. I mean, you've told me dozens of times what she says. So now she's gone off to do her own thing. So?"

"You are absolutely the most heartless and unfeeling human being I have ever known in my life. If you're even a human being at all!"

"Because I don't believe in this old 'bloodline' garbage?"

"Because you don't seem to care about—I don't think you care about anything or anyone enough to miss *anything*. I miss her, I tell you. I keep thinking about her and how she flew kites with us, and she laughs a lot, or anyway used to, and how she suddenly hugs me and says, 'Love you, Taylor.' I miss it. *I miss her*," she said through an intolerable ache in her throat.

"You're acting as if she were dead. She's just gone away, maybe only for a while anyway."

"Oh, I have a feeling," Taylor said tonelessly. "I have a feeling deep inside me that it isn't going to be just for a while. Once she gets—gets free—I don't think she'll be able to come back. I think you could just as soon expect one of those fish of Jem's to swim back and beg for the tank again once he's let them loose. That's what I think."

"Well, *I* still don't think it's the end of the world. In fact, maybe you'll have the best of two worlds, huh? You can live here where you've got Tony and the birds and Jem and B.J. and me, and you can go up to New York City once in a while and hell it up with your mother. She'll probably go all glamorous and be quite exciting."

"Junie thinks glamor is silly."

"Wait and see."

"How do you know she'll want me?"

"Oh, don't be a dope, Taylor. Anyone who's been around you people knows your mother's crazy about her kids. I wouldn't be surprised if she was still crazy about Tony, you know. It's just that she can't take being married anymore. I, personally, am never going to be married, what with the examples I see all around me."

Taylor sniffed. "What about the Dobkins?"

"All those *kids*. Yuck. Happiness isn't worth it." Sandy frowned into the sunlight. "There's one thing though."

"What?"

"She'll have to make a living, won't she? I mean, Tony's not rich, and I betcha he won't give her alimony."

"They aren't divorced *yet*," Taylor snapped.

"No, but it's like you said. I think you're right—once a woman gets away, she won't come back. Only how does somebody her age, who's only been a housewife, make a living?"

~~*fourteen*

Junie's letter came a few days later, on Saturday. It was addressed only to Tony, and he had already left for work. Taylor and Jem put it on the table, next to the undisturbed note and the telegram, and all day their eyes kept coming back to it. The return address was to June Bellamy, in some town in Connecticut neither of them had heard of.

"June Bellamy," Taylor said sourly. "*You* remember her—old Judge Bellamy's doting daughter."

Jem, who'd planned to fish, changed his mind, as if the letter somehow anchored him to the house. Taylor refused an invitation to come over and glom Alexander.

"Glom?" she said to Sandy.

191

"I've been reading Dashiell Hammett. He's marvelous. In those days you glommed people."

"How did they look when you'd finished?"

"Oh, Taylor, it meant just to look at them. Slang. I like it. Come on, come over."

"No. There's a letter from Junie here."

"It won't fly away if you come here for a swim and a glom."

"You can't tell," Taylor said gravely. "It just might."

"Why don't you open it?"

"It's addressed to Tony."

"Steam it open."

"Sandy, I'm going to hang up on you," Taylor said, and did.

But neither she nor Jem could figure what to do with themselves between now and midnight. B.J. was in the shallow waters by the dock, playing with Drum. They hoped he'd stay for a long time, since the moment he came out he'd start whining. He had stopped wailing aloud for his mother, but was in a constant state of irritability. One night he'd wet the bed, something he hadn't done in over a year, and had screamed at Jem, who was changing the sheets, that the whole thing was his fault.

"You made me!" he yelled at his brother. "You did it!"

"Ah, pipe down," Jem said, but his voice was not

really impatient.

Taylor gave B.J. a bath and put him in the freshly made bed and sat beside him, smoothing his back rhythmically until he fell asleep.

She'd gone out on the porch, where Jem was sitting on the swing, pushing it slowly back and forth. "We have to tell Tony," she said. "This is getting worse, not better."

"Yeah."

"Well, are we going to?"

"Sure, Taylor. Let's wait a bit. Give her—give things a little longer. The mosquitoes are awful. I'm going in."

On Saturday they circled the table with the letter on it, and finally Jem said, "I got an idea."

"What?"

"Let's clean the house."

Taylor blinked. "The whole place?"

"Yup. We'll start with the kitchen and keep steppin'."

When they'd removed everything from the spice and canned fruit shelf, an assortment of various-sized palmetto bugs scurried about, frenzied at this disturbance.

Grandmother Reddick: Call them palmetto bugs if you think it makes them less offensive, but those things are cockroaches.

193

Tony: But palmetto bug sounds better, don't you think? I read somewhere that they're actually quite clean.

Grandmother Reddick: In Massachusetts they are cockroaches, and they're dirty.

Jem and Taylor could not bring themselves to swat bugs, and anyway there were too many for that. Jem unearthed, from beneath the sink, one of their grandmother's powerful insecticides. Then he and his sister took every jar, bottle, carton and can from the cupboards, washed the shelves and applied insecticide as liberally as Grandmother Reddick ever had.

"If there's anything left alive in here, including us, by the time we're finished," said Jem, "I'll be very surprised."

They dragged from beneath the counter all the pots and pans. Most were filmed with grease.

"Here's a whole bunch more of these fellows," Jem said, squatting. "A flourishing commune of *cucarachas*. Well, here goes, guys. Sorry." He looked at his sister. "Why don't we ever do this in between when Grandmother's here?"

Taylor shrugged. She was sweaty and hot. She could feel dirty streams of sweat running down her body. But the filthier she and Jem became, the more magically marvelous became their kitchen, and when they were finished they stood in the doorway, transfixed with wonder.

They'd left the closet doors open so that when Tony came in he'd be able to see the glorious transformation. Everywhere everything snapped and sparkled, shone with spotless purity.

Taylor looked at the kitchen clock. It, too, had had its face washed. Six-thirty. "My God, Jem. Where's B.J.?"

"Don't panic," he said, racing outside. He turned back at the porch door. "Asleep on the swing, with Tut on top and Drum beside. He's okay if they don't smother him."

"I'm going to take a shower."

"Okay. I'll wait and see that he doesn't wake up and think *we've* gone off and left him. Let's let the rest of the house go until tomorrow." He looked at the kitchen again. "I kind of hate to use it, don't you? It'll never be like this again."

Taylor went out on the porch when she'd showered, and sat opposite B.J., studying his face, gentle and dear in sleep. Poor little thing, she thought. Poor motherless boy. Drum was so close that B.J. was crowded to the back of the swing. Tut was on the porch railing now, eying an apple-green lizard about the size of his tail tip. The lizard stood high on its little webbed feet a few yards from the cat. Tut could have had it in a second but was apparently too lazy to move. Did the lizard sense this? Taylor wondered. If so, it suddenly decided not to push its luck. It dropped eight feet from the railing to the sand and disappeared under the house.

I wonder how he stands this heat, Taylor thought, looking at the sleeping B.J. He was flushed, his hair wet and curly from perspiration, his mouth open a little.

He sighed, flung himself around, found his face buried in Drum's side and woke up. Taylor braced herself for the uproar, but none came. Her brother lay there, drenched from sleeping under such crowded circumstances, and smiled at her.

He doesn't remember, she thought. Smiling now, but just wait till he remembers.

"Want to jump in the water?" she said. "Drum's got you all hot and sweaty."

B.J. didn't reply. He lay back and looked at the thin boards of the porch ceiling, pushed at Drum ineffectually, gave up, and closed his eyes again. Taylor reached over and took Drum by the scruff of the neck, easing him off the swing.

When Jem came out she pointed at B.J. "He's still asleep. Do you think he's sick? He looks sort of red. Maybe it's just from sleeping with the animals."

"He looks okay to me," Jem said. "Just sweaty." He glanced at the bay. "High tide. He could have a swim when he wakes up."

"I've already suggested it. He just went back to sleep."

"What do you want for supper, Taylor? And don't say nothing. I'm tired of fixing food you don't eat. You have to start eating. Now. Tonight. I'll make an omelet."

He's right, she thought. It's sort of—punishing people, not to eat. An omelet was an easy start. "That'd be nice," she said.

"Good. You just watch the firecracker here, see he doesn't go off. I'll get supper. I sure hate to muck up that kitchen," he said, going into the house.

B.J., when he woke for the second time, sat up and said, "You know something, Taylor?"

"What, B.J.?"

"I'll be sorry when you die."

"Well—"

"Tony will die before you. I'll be sorry when he dies."

"Well, B.J.—"

"I'll be sorry when Drum dies. And Tut. And Vicky."

"Vicky? Oh, at the supermarket."

"Yes. I'll be sorry when Mr. Simonson dies."

"Who's Mr. Simonson?"

"Somebody I know that you don't. I'll be sorry

when he dies." He paused, turning over other prospects. "I'll be sorry when Jem dies. And Sandy. Well—maybe not so much. But I'll be sorry when Viva dies."

"B.J.!"

"I'll be sorry when I die. But by then I'll probably have some children, won't I, Taylor?"

"Maybe."

"I'll have a couple of boys. They'll be sorry when I die."

"B.J.! Listen to me!"

"What, Taylor?"

"Why don't you jump in the water? You're hot and covered with sweat and—"

"Taylor?"

"What, B.J.?"

"Did Junie die?"

"Oh, B.J., *no*. She just went on a trip. To New York City."

"Is that far?"

"Pretty far. But not very."

"Why didn't she say good-bye?"

"You were asleep. She tried to say good-bye, but you didn't wake up."

Since this happened often enough, B.J. seemed to accept it. "When is she coming home?"

"I'm not sure."

He stood up. "I guess I'll go in the water." He peeled off his trunks and dove naked off the dock. Drum was right behind him.

∽∽

It really was one of the hottest nights Taylor could remember. They got B.J. to bed with Drum on the floor beside him and an electric fan aimed straight at him. He surprised them by going to sleep without a protest.

"Maybe he is sick," Jem said thoughtfully. "He hasn't yelled at us all day."

"I think he's just tired out. From so much emotion." They glanced at the table where the unopened letter lay. "I know I'm tired from it," she said.

"Let's look at the movie, the one about the car killing people."

"We've already seen it. It's dopey."

"I know. But I think I'll look anyway."

Taylor sat beside him on the floor, looking at the dopey thing. During one of the advertisements, she said, "Remember Whizzer?"

"That gerbil? What about him? Or her?"

"I don't know. I was just thinking about her. Or him."

They had never known the sex of the gerbil. It had been B.J.'s adored pet and had lived in a cage in his room, opposite Jem's tanks. It had a little wheel to

199

run around in, and an upstairs suite fluffy with torn newspaper, and now and then, with the door closed, a spell of freedom. One morning B.J. had got up to find his gerbil dead.

He'd sat on the floor, holding it in his hands, crying, crooning, sobbing. Without, it appeared, any hope of ever being comforted. It had been Jem who suggested they give Whizzer a sea burial.

Tears running down his face, B.J. had looked up and gasped, "How?"

"I'll show you."

Whizzer was laid on a bit of velvet in a clean Crisco can weighted with pebbles, and Taylor had collected some hibiscus blossoms. Tony took them out on the Gulf of Mexico on *Loon*. He blew his horn for the bridge keeper and they motored through the pass, B.J. looking important, as he always did when the bridge went up for *Loon* and cars had to wait on either side. Once past the bridge, Tony cut the motor, Jem got the sail up, and they'd run before the breeze, heeling a little. Drum, standing in the bow, had that smile that dogs seem to get, facing into the wind.

When they were well under way, Tony told Jem to drop the sail and they rocked there on the gently lifting waters while B.J. eased the Crisco can with its beloved burden over the side. Taylor scattered the hibiscus flowers, Jem ran the sail up again. They were still floating, the hisbiscus blossoms, brilliant sun-colored cups, when Tony came about and headed home.

B.J. cried quietly and solemnly all the way, but when they leaped from *Loon* there was Junie, holding a kitten, a small striped pumpkin-colored pussycat that she held out for B.J.'s tear-stained inspection.

He took one look, one gulp, and fell in love. He never mentioned Whizzer again. And, for that matter, he did not now pay much attention to Tut, matured into a large pumpkin-colored striped cat. Drum was B.J.'s familiar. Taylor wished him a good long life, because as B.J. got older he wouldn't find it so easy to be solaced for the loss of a friend with a sea burial and a kitten.

"I'm so *hot*," Taylor said now. "Why don't you turn that dumb thing off? It's stupid."

"Okay." Jem eased over, clicked off the television set. "We could go up and turn on the air conditioner in Grandmother's room."

"I don't like air-conditioning."

"Well, I can't order a storm for you. I know, let's swim."

"We can't. What if he woke up?"

"For Pete's sake, we're right outside the house."

"But he's at the front and we'll be way at the back."

"Suit yourself. I'm gonna swim."

Like B.J., Jem simply pulled off his shorts and

walked unconcernedly naked out on the dock. Taylor hesitated, but could almost hear her mother's voice. "Taylor, there is no call to be ashamed of a normal human body doing its normal job of developing. Go and swim."

Taylor pulled off her shirt and shorts and ran after her brother. The tide was coming in, but still they had to go all the way to the end of the dock for deep water. A long way from the front of the house, Taylor thought as she did a surface dive and swam through schools of needlefish. She went as far as she could under water before springing into the air, shouting with pleasure. They dove and surfaced and slithered like eels. They dog-paddled, moving their hands so that phosphorescent ctenophores gleamed in the dark, glowed in eerie outlines along their limbs. They floated, face down, face up.

After a long happy while, Jem swam to the ladder and climbed up, Taylor following. They got into their clothes not bothering with towels, letting their skin and hair drip. There was no sound from B.J., but Taylor said she thought she'd go in and take a look at him anyway. "Be right back," she told Jem.

She did not turn on the light, even in the hall, for fear of waking him, and then stumbled over him in the dark.

B.J. woke with a yell of fright that turned into a scream of rage when Taylor had switched on the lamp to see where he was.

"You been out! You been swimming and left me all alone here with ghosties—"

"Ghosties? Oh, come on, B.J."

"White things coming in the window!"

Taylor tried for a lie. "We didn't go swimming—"

"You're lying you're lying you're lying! Your hair's all wet and you're wet all over and you been swimming!"

Jem appeared in the doorway, looking resigned. "What the heck is it now?"

"I was just trying to tell him that we didn't go far—" Taylor began, "but I can't get through all the hollering. B.J.! We were only at the end of the dock, only for a few minutes!"

"You went and left me all alone!"

"But we're back. And you didn't even know you were alone until I fell over you. How can you yell at us for something you didn't even know was going on?"

"This is interesting," said Jem. "You're trying to carry on a sensible conversation with a nitwit."

"If I didn't wake up then I wouldn't know," B.J. screamed at Taylor. "But you *kicked* me and that's how I know and you aren't *supposed* to leave me alone and I'm gonna tell on you!"

"I didn't kick you, you mutt. I stumbled over you. Why don't you stay in bed where you belong?"

"It's too hot in bed. You kicked me and I'm gonna tell Junie on you." He stopped. "Did she come back yet?"

"Well, no. Not yet, B.J."

B.J., a moment before loud and upright in rage, crumpled. He crawled back on his bed, shoved himself into the corner near the wall and cried with his face in the sheets.

Taylor and Jem stood in the doorway. Guarding him against ghosties? Taylor wondered. The ghosties were dream things and would be forgotten. Would B.J. forget Junie if she didn't come back?

Tony, coming home, found his children like this. Two of them standing at the bedroom door, not speaking, the third sobbing in the corner of a crumpled bed.

~~fifteen

"Come on, B.J.," Tony said, gathering his son in his arms. "Let's take you in the bathroom and give you a nice shower, and then we'll all go in and have something to eat, how's that? I brought home some pâté de maison, made by yours truly and widely highly thought of if I do say so, and some strawberries the size of your fist. How about it?"

Waiting in the living room, because the mosquitoes were too bad on the porch, Taylor said to Jem, "He must be awfully tired."

"Yeah."

"Should we give him the letter, or just let him find it?"

"I suppose we better give it to him."

"Before or after we have the snack?"

"I don't want a snack."

"I guess neither does he. It's his impulse to feed people when— Well, it's what he thinks of. If I can get something down, you can."

"Okay."

Tony came in, B.J. in his arms. "Okay, kids. You haven't made a start on the feast? Well, looks like it's up to us, fella," he said to B.J., whose head was lolling on his shoulder. He smiled at the other two and laid his son gently on the sofa. B.J. was asleep at once.

"What started all that?" Tony asked.

"We went for a swim," Taylor said. "Just off the dock. He wouldn't even have known except he'd fallen out of bed, or got out of bed, and I fell over him when I went in to check."

Tony scratched his cheek. It sounded raspy. He was faintly bearded as always at the end of a working day. His eyes looked deep, his skin white under its tan. When he said, "Is he having a hard time? Giving you two a hard time?" Taylor's impulse was to tell him everything was fine. But everything wasn't, and she and Jem weren't handling things well, and—

"It's awful, Tony," said Jem.

Their father sat down and looked at them. He rubbed his forehead, stretching the skin tight. "I guess we'll have to do something about it."

"There's a letter there," said Taylor. "It came this morning."

She thought her father's face whitened even more. She thought, for a moment, he was just going to let the envelope lie there and not touch it. But after a long time he leaned forward and picked it up, opened it and read.

Taylor and Jem waited, taking quick shallow breaths. I'm afraid, Taylor thought. This feeling—it's being afraid.

Tony folded the letter and put it back in the envelope, dropped the envelope on the table. He looked around the room in a spent, aimless way. His eyes came to the intaglio of the fish that had killed each other and died locked together. He closed his lids.

Taylor, in a panic, looked at Jem, who was chewing at his thumbnail and staring back at her.

"Tony!"

He stirred, opened his eyes. "Yeah, sure. Okay, kids—this is how it stands—" He cleared his throat, coughed, exhaled a long sighing whistling breath. "This is how it stands—"

They waited.

"How it stands," he resumed, "is she's going to study to be a legal secretary. There in old Uncle Jim's office. So she'll have to learn to type after all, eh? She says she may even go to school at night and study law." He grinned hideously. "A lawyer, like her daddy."

"She can't do that!" Jem said. "She's too old!"

Taylor felt a spurt of defensive anger. Junie had a college degree. She wasn't that old. Why shouldn't she go to school at night and study law? How she wanted to get away from us, she thought. All this time and we never knew how *much* she wanted to get away. ("She's told you in fifty thousand ways," said the voice of Sandy in her mind. "In fifty thousand ways.")

"Are you gonna get divorced?" Jem asked. As if that was what mattered, thought Taylor. "Are you, Tony?" Jem insisted.

"She doesn't say anything about that. She says she hopes with all—with all her *heart*—that we'll understand and—forgive her. She says she hopes she can come here to see us, and that you will go to see her. In New York City."

"No *way*," said Jem.

They were, the two of them, so angry, so wounded. They might never forgive her. Gentle Tony and sweet-humored Jem were, at this moment, boiling with pain and rage and Taylor wondered if they ever would get over it.

What I should be surprised at, she thought, is why I'm not boiling with rage and pain. Maybe some of Sandy's ways have rubbed off on me, and I really don't care what they do, grown-ups who have kids and change their minds and louse up everyone's life. Maybe I really don't care what she does.

"Look," Tony said. "I've been thinking. Would you two mind very much if I asked my mother to come down here? Just for a while, just till we can figure something out. I mean, school will be starting, and B.J. *needs* somebody—"

Don't cry, Tony, Taylor thought. Please don't cry, or we'll all fly apart and maybe never find the pieces.

He didn't. He rubbed his mustache, with both index fingers. Rubbed it long and carefully while he composed himself. "Well," he said. "What about it?"

"Do you think she'll come?" Taylor asked. "Grandmother hates Florida in the summer."

"She'll come, if I ask. My mother—she's a homebody, let's call it. A family type. You know. I just want to know if you two will get along with her?"

Here she comes, radiating pot roasts.

"It's okay with us," Jem said. Tony didn't appear to notice that he'd answered for both of them.

Here she comes, radiating standards.

Well, it wouldn't kill them. B.J. would love it.

After Tony had put a sleeping B.J. back to bed and he and Jem had gone to their rooms, Taylor stored the pâté de maison and the strawberries that really were as big as fists, if the fists were small, in the icebox. The kitchen was super clean. She hoped Tony would notice in the morning.

Passing Jem's room, she heard soft sobbing. B.J. awake again? Crying in his sleep?

"Junie . . . Oh, *Mom* . . ."

Not B.J. Jem, crying in the dark that was beginning to pale toward dawn. Taylor walked on and upstairs. There was nothing she could do for Jem.

Her parents' door was open. The room dark. Was Tony asleep, or just lying there? Ought she to go in to him? She decided not, went along the hall and saw a crack of light under Grandmother's door.

For a long time she stood, hand lifted, hesitating. Finally she knocked.

"Okay," he called. "I'm not asleep."

The air-conditioning was on. The room was cool, even a little cold. Tony was lying on the bed, still dressed, staring upward, hands beneath his head. His face in the lamplight was expressionless. How could she know what was going on in his mind? Or in Jem's, or B.J.'s? She wasn't sure about herself, what she was thinking, what she felt. Tired, anyway.

"Tony?"

"Yes, honey?"

"Can I come in for a bit?"

"Of course."

She crossed the room, sat in a little chintz-covered armchair. Grandmother had sent it down from Massachusetts, along with the sleigh bed Tony was on now.

"Sometimes," she said, "I wish people had those balloons coming out of their heads. You know, like the funny papers. So you could tell what they were thinking."

"You only think you wish it. You can be grateful those balloons only come out of the heads of people in funny papers."

"I see." After a while, she said, "It's nice and cool in here. It was a good idea for you to—" She didn't finish that thought. He was here because he wouldn't go into the room he'd shared with Junie. He didn't have to send a balloon out of his head to tell her that.

"Are you angry?" she said nervously, not able to keep from asking.

Tony looked at her for the first time since she'd come into the room. "Taylor, I'm not much of a poetry reader, but I've been remembering a poem I read once, way back, a long time ago. I only remember one line. It was by Robert Frost. He said, 'We love the things we love for what they are.' Do you know what that means?"

"Could you tell me?"

"I don't think he was talking about things only—except I imagine he meant those, too. But he also meant people and plants and ideas and—hell, maybe coromandel screens. I think he meant you don't love in spite of anything or because of anything. You just love what you love. For what it is, the way it is. I love your mother. I think it's possible to come to the end of loving, but right now—yes, I love her. I'm—what she's doing to us—" He sighed heavily.

"What if she comes back?"

Her father's expression, which had been thoughtful, grew cold and closed.

"Love is one thing," he said at length. "Understanding—trying to, that's another. But forgiving—Don't ask me that, Taylor. Not yet. I'm not ready to answer that yet. I'll tell you this—if she walked in the room right now I think I'd kill her. I wouldn't, of course, but I'd want to kill her. It's a good thing, right now, that she's far away, out of my reach. Go to bed, Taylor."

She stood up. She wanted to kiss him, but didn't. At the door, she turned. "You should get some sleep, too."

"I will."

"I mean, get undressed and go to bed and *sleep*."

"I will."

She wavered at the sill. "Well, good night."

He nodded. She closed the door and went on up to her own room.

Once, early in the summer, they'd all been over at the beach, making a sand castle. Not a great project like the one that had been in the newspaper, but a good elaborate castle just the same.

Suddenly Junie had cried out, "Look! Look *quickly*!"

A school of flying fish flashed by, skimming the surface of the waves like a flock of great silver-blue dragonflies. They dazzled and were gone. You had to be looking at just the right moment, to see flying fish, and then you were never sure you really had—even though you knew you had—it was a sight so bright, beautiful, brief.

B.J. had jumped up and down, clutching Jem's arm. "Jem! Catch one, *catch* one! You can put him in your tank!"

"No way," said Jem.

"Why *not*?"

"I couldn't catch one. They're too speedy. If I did catch one, it wouldn't be beautiful anymore. It'd be ugly. They're only beautiful out there, racing over the waves. Some fish you can keep in a tank, B.J. Only not those."

For a while longer they looked at the ocean, at the place where the sparkling host had been and was no longer. After that, Taylor remembered, we got back to building a wall around our castle, to keep it safe until the tide came in.

MARY STOLZ

One of today's most distinguished and versatile writers, Mary Stolz is the author of more than forty books that have been enjoyed by over a million young readers. *Atlantic Monthly* calls her "one of the most rewarding writers for teenagers." Among her many honors, she was nominated for the 1975 National Book Award for her novel THE EDGE OF NEXT YEAR and has had several of her books chosen as ALA Notable Children's Books, including most recently CAT IN THE MIRROR.

Born in Boston and educated at the Birch Wathen School and Columbia University in New York City, Mary Stolz now lives with her husband, Dr. Thomas C. Jaleski, in Florida.

Format by Gloria Bressler
Set in 12 pt. Garamond
Composed, printed and bound by Vail-Ballou Press, Inc.
HARPER & ROW, PUBLISHERS, INCORPORATED